WATER

Jasper Joffe

WATER

TELEGRAM

British Library Cataloguing-in-Publication Data
A catalogue record for this book is available from the British Library

ISBN 1-84659-004-3
EAN 9-781846-590047

copyright © Jasper Joffe, 2006

This edition published 2006 by Telegram Books

TELEGRAM
26 Westbourne Grove
London W2 5RH
www.telegrambooks.com

Foreword

All first novels are autobiographical is perhaps the most boring thing you could ever say in the world. And I hate this jocular first-person style. Repetition is tragedy, repeated as farce, repeated as boredom, repeated as pomposity etc, etc.

I was telling a friend about this book, that the theme was that even though you love someone you can still mess it all up. And she started crying. So I think it must be a good story, or maybe she was just thinking about something else.

My name is Nathaniel Water and I want this to be the best novel you have ever read because it is about me and I am the most interesting person I have ever met. I am introduced to people with so-called first-class minds all the time and they are most often stupid and not amusing to talk to. In contrast, I am always thinking about what would entertain the people I am with, and worrying about what they are thinking. That's part of why I am so interesting (as well as, of course, because I am preternaturally talented).

An autobiographical novel? Well, yes and no. This is really not what happened. But I refuse not to enjoy and exalt my life, and I will not renounce one thing I have done, so I have put it all into this book. My second wife used to get enraged when I told her I loved life (she would have preferred I told her I loved *her*, but she and I wore those words out), but it is true, I do love life; I read in an Isaac Bashevis Singer story that of all lies the greatest falsehood is melancholy. Life must be got on with because death is relatively imminent, and as far as I know that will mean non-existence. Even when I am totally miserable and nihilistic, I usually see some tiny thing on the tube or on TV which makes me laugh – confirming the greatness of life.

I married two women. Imagine one beautiful, Slovakian and difficult; the other, pretty, successful, German and normal. I wasn't a bigamist, or bigmatic if that is the adjective, but the two marriages were in close enough proximity to raise questions about my judgement. Both wives became pregnant because they wanted children and I think sex is better without a safety net. Only one gave birth. I left each of my wives at least once, and I deserted them both when they were weak and in hospital. I hate repetition, as I have said before, but I am always doing the same things over and over again. I pursued and married these women because I had to do something with my life when I wasn't painting, and marriage was the most daring (stupidest) option for someone who gets bored easily.

Don't read this next bit too carefully. When you try and say anything general about art it always comes out dumb and easy to contradict. Perhaps you should even skip to Chapter One.

I will tell this story in the third person. 'Nathaniel Water was an artist. He painted pictures, etcetera.' I hope this makes it clear that this is not my, Nathaniel Water's, story, but something more than that. I have racked my brain to dredge up memories, and forced myself to listen to my friends so I can steal their stories. I have even gone so far as to attend long and boring parties in order to glimpse a little bit of actuality. It is with great effort that I have augmented the splendid facts of my life to create the richer tapestry of fiction. I believe all art stems from its variation from reality. Take a painting of an apple: its most important quality is that it is flat whilst the apple is not. This illusion, or gap between one thing and another, is in the first instance what makes the painting interesting. Of course all painting is abstract and figurative at the same time. And that is its eternal, internal variation.

I hope I'm not losing you. Don't worry; although this is the story of an artist, there aren't too many boring bits about art.

I love the word 'boring'. Boring people say that only boring people say things are boring.

There's much more about passionate, tragic love, and my rise to the heady heights of the art world – that beautiful journey towards great success, which is always pretty much the same in any business and therefore relevant to everyone who hankers after it.

Don't get confused if the story jumps around sometimes. There are only a few main characters. The rest are just walk-ons who don't matter much.

The principals are:

Nathaniel Water the painter that is I.

Harriet the German curator whom I marry after I have been engaged to Jelena.

Jelena the Slovakian writer whom I marry after I divorce Harriet.

And my family, who created much of what I am.

I have started the story with an interesting bit where I am arguing with Jelena. After that I am thinking about marrying her. Go figure!

1

I think of arguing and it seems like it's what I like to do because I am always disagreeing with everyone, then I remember that it's why it was so awful with Jelena. Then I know that I fell in love with her because she was so difficult, and I always want what I can't have. And I remember the shouting, and it doesn't seem so bad. But then I think shouting is violence. I saw a newspaper article about abused husbands and I thought of myself, which seems a little melodramatic. It's hard to recreate the horror and hatred of screaming and shouting. And I have some friends who say they never argue and can't imagine what we find to argue about. And I say, 'Nothing really.'

He spoke in an even, low voice. 'You are a fucking anorexic bitch with no talent, and I hate you, you cunt, I hate your family, your mother and your father, and your stupid dog. You're so boring, you just say the same thing over and over again. You talk about yourself all the time and you moan. You love rich people and the only reason you're with me is because I'm famous. Otherwise you'd be with some rich businessman Italian fucking idiot, who'd take you out to dinner and listen to your crap. But you're too scared to do what you want.'

'You want to destroy me, psychopath!' she screamed. 'You stingy Jewish. Schizophrenic lady. You're jealous of my friends, also my dog. You *pezzo di stronzo*. I prefer my other boyfriends because they're not sadists. You want me locked up in a mental hospital. You want to kill me. You want to kill me. You want to kill me. You're weak.'

He held the phone away from his ear; his head had no more room for her anger.

Water thought it an interesting idea for he and Jelena to be as nasty to each other as possible. They had tried tolerance and promising not to argue. Self-control didn't work, so now they, he more than she, said the worst things they could think of. Charles had sent them an American self-help book called *Communication Miracles for Couples*. A gift which Jelena had found funny, and Water insulting. They had arrived instead at a communication holocaust.

'We've given up being nice to each other. I just say what I want to her. I'm sick of pretending. It seems to be working.' When Water told this to one of his friends, there was a patronising silence indicating that Water was so deluded that a look of pity was the only appropriate response.

'You are a prostitute. A fucking whore, and a liar. All you want is men telling you that you look pretty and buying you dinner. So you had a few boyfriends in your life. Big deal. I've had more relationships in one year than you've had in your whole life.'

'Homosexual. Feminine lady. I only lied to you because you are not a man. Leave me alone. You destroyed my friends in Rome, my family, my *carriera*, just because you're jealous, and have no balls. You lady!' She was screaming again so he put the phone down and called her back. She picked it up, answered in a normal voice, heard it was him, put it down. He rang her again; she picked it up, and asked him to call her back on her mobile.

'Listen,' he said.

'I can't hear you.'

'Can you hear me now?'

'Yes.'

'You know why I am doing this?' How ugly these expressions were, but he had decided not to care about that anymore.

'No.'

'Because I got sick of always being positive, while you moaned – sick of convincing you that you should believe in me, of arguing with your doubts. If I'm an optimist, you are a pessimist in response.'

'I can't hear you.'

'You never can hear me when I say anything important.' He spluttered with anger. In calmer moments Water wondered whether by 'hear' she actually meant 'listen to'. He hung up and phoned her back on her home line.

'Can you hear me now?' He had forgotten what he was angry about. She sounded worn out.

'Yes,' she said.

'So?'

'Oh nothing. Listen. I love you, that's all. I just want you to decide you love me too. Can you hear me?'

She laughed in a pretty way.

'I decided a long time ago. But you insult me every time. I cannot forgive you, I don't forget very easy like you.'

'What did you decide?' he said.

'That we are together.'

'But in what way? I live here. You live there. You spend all your time with other people, me too. We are not together.' She had said the same thing to him once.

'OK, we're not together. You could have stayed and lived here.'

'For fuck's sake, you know why I didn't. Let's not go through history again. I want you to decide to be with me. Now. Or leave me alone,' he said.

'I can't hear you.'

'Can you hear me now?'

'Yes.'

'Let's go. I've had enough. You don't get it. It's enough. I'll phone you sometime,' he said.

He felt quite good, being nasty and angry all the time. Perhaps it was his real personality, the one you grew into as you got older. When he was good, Jelena was bad. So why not be bad? Jelena was happy for other reasons at that time, selling stories to magazines and with firm hopes for the future. She didn't seem to notice Water had lost – or given up – control. It was, to her, just the progression of his previous character.

'Hello. How are you? This is Water.'

'I got it. I'm very busy. Yesterday I had to interview three different people. I was all round Rome. Everybody was making me crazy. Tomorrow I am going to Milan to talk to a man who is starting a new magazine. It's terrible; I don't know if he wants me to write regularly or just one feature. I don't care. He is an idiot. I haven't had any sleep. Tonight I am going to Rosa's for dinner. She's making homemade fettuccini. Like you hated.'

'I didn't hate it. I quite liked it. So when will we meet?' he said.

'I can't think about it now. Too busy with this circus. Once I know about Milan. Then you can come here, or I'll go home to my parents. I don't know. I am crazy here, nowhere to stay.'

'OK. OK. So let me know when you know more. How come

you didn't sleep? What did you do last night?' He had phoned the night before and she had been out. Her mobile had been switched off.

'I just went for a pizza and drank one beer.'

'With whom?'

'The German.'

'I thought you said he was creepy.'

No reply.

'Was it just the two of you? Why did you go out with him?'

'What does it matter? You interrogate me like my mother. I have to feel guilty because I want to eat dinner? I was back by 9.45.'

'But why with him? You said he was creepy. Then you go on another date with him.'

'He phoned. I told him I was leaving Rome and was busy. Then he phoned later, so we ate one pizza near my house. I paid for it. Eighteen euros. You want me to sit crying in my room.'

'I can't believe you. You just don't give a shit. This guy wants to fuck you. And you are eating dinner with him. You betray me. After we argue you rush out to meet some fucking creepy idiot. Maybe you're not unfaithful to me physically, but it's ugly what you do, vulgar, laughing at me. Dancing on our grave. I've had enough. Really. We're finished. OK. I am finished with you.'

Water's jealousy strangled his reason and wrenched his stomach. No matter how much information he forced from her, he could never know why it all happened.

I hate this silly jealousy. It seems like a joke from this distance. Now when I am no longer with her, I cannot imagine why I should have been so jealous. Perhaps she provoked it, or it could have just been because we were apart. I know that I will be jealous again with or without reason.

2

Visiting Jelena in Rome, where Water had once lived. Vulgar chapter about real life, written in a dull chronological manner. Needs to be broken up by witty self-conscious voice.

Two bottles of Laurent Perrier champagne. It was a neutral present. Too many gifts had lessened the amusement to be had from them. Champagne was usually fun to drink together though. He had taken a taxi to his early morning flight. Cheap tickets were scarce; planes were overloaded by too many English tourists, enjoying their sterling power and the results of the competitive short-haul market.

For a well-off artist it was amazing how little money he had most of the time. He was always waiting to be paid and spending too much money in advance, but it was hardly like he was starving to death in Africa, he reminded himself. Frequent flying had left him fatigued at the thought of more airport processes. Familiarity had even dulled the thrill of fear. From London to Rome it all took about eight hours door to door, from waking up to putting his bag down on the tiled floor of her room.

He finished in the duty free, more expensive than the taxed prices in Italy, then waited to board the plane, which was late, and at whose gate long queues had already formed. The ticketless airline did not allocate seats and therefore created anxiety amongst the waiting passengers that there might be too few, or perhaps they just wanted to get the best ones, but he sat reading his Russian novel, indicating his superiority by his refusal to join the crowd.

On the plane he sat at the back (where more people survived). The earliness of the flight meant he was tired enough to sleep for most of its two-hour duration. He wanted to magically arrive in Italy without awareness of more dull time passing, like when children hope that they might sleep until Christmas Day. He didn't even take much notice of the long spells of turbulence signalling hot weather on the way. Waking up, he went back to sleep. There was nothing you could do: the plane normally stayed floating in the sky no matter how much it shook. A soft landing, then another tedious delay as the steps were connected to allow disembarkation. He felt the warmth of the Roman day as soon he was out of the plane, but the sky was cloudy, not as clear as he had hoped.

The airport was not the busy main one so the luggage was quickly moved onto the conveyor belt. He called Jelena from a payphone using a telephone card he had left over from another trip. He said he would meet her at the train station, but that the plane had been an hour late, so he would be too and he was sorry about that. He got on the airline bus which was more expensive than the train/metro option but less hassle. It was stuffy, making him feel like he couldn't breathe – the same sensation he had had on the plane, which must have been caused by the unusual atmospheric pressure, he reasoned. In England that morning the taxi's windows had been shut and the heater turned on. A storm was coming. He had suffocated in silence, not wishing to engage in any way with the driver who controlled the electric windows.

Nothing worse than hearing an anecdote by someone who believes they're good at telling stories. Not even much of an anecdote this. Jelena is always fucking late, which is annoying. And I remember her friend telling me that if anyone else is late Jelena gets angry/ hysterical. I am mostly very punctual, usually early, but actually I enjoy waiting for people. It's often more fun than being with them.

The bus was boring: a woman speaking badly-pronounced English attempted to sell the passengers guided tours of Rome, perhaps the real profit to be made from the bus service. He was surprised that a few people handed over money there and then for tour tickets (tourists taking tours not that strange actually, he thought afterwards). When the bus reached the main railway station he pushed his way off and sprinted towards Platform Two where he had agreed to meet her, exactly an hour late. She was not there so he searched around a little then called her on her mobile. 'Hello. I'm here.' 'I am in a bookshop,' she said. 'I'll meet you at the front of the station.' The station was busy in a way he liked. From the front you could appreciate the magnificence of its great wave-shaped roof, it was a good place to meet your girlfriend. The waiting was pleasurable now, anticipating the first sight was delicious, worth drawing out. Scanning the crowds from the vantage point of a wall warmed by sunshine, he appreciated the style of Rome's inhabitants. They were well-dressed and many were good-looking. Twenty minutes passed, and his pleasure became impatience, so he phoned her again. She was somewhere in the station. He told her again to meet him at the front. A few minutes later he spotted her from a distance. She had had her hair dyed. It was two colours: brown and gold, a look that surprised him. She was thinner and more tanned than he remembered her. They kissed hello awkwardly. He didn't know what to say but tried to remain positive. 'How is my hair?' she asked. 'It's OK. Good,' he replied. She wore a black skirt and sleeveless top. They walked to her scooter, not saying much. He was measuring his emotions, hoping his feelings would speak certainly about her.

She asked what he wanted to do: go to a park, which she had told him much about on the telephone, or eat something. Or go to her shared flat to drop his bags. They drove to a café which she liked and he had never been to. At a plastic table, outside under a trellis roof, they shared an ice cream, he drank a Coke and she a Campari and soda. He felt better as the sugar surged through him. He went to the cramped toilet to wash his face. The people at other tables seemed aware that he and she were speaking English. She told him that she liked this café because the red and black plastic tables made a pattern, and he talked a little about the beautiful clouded skies over the motorway.

He looked at her arm and touched it, then stopped, not wanting to be too much too soon. He paid and she said they should take a little walk around the small market in the square, and that he might be interested in the area as a good place to buy an apartment. It was quite nice, but the differences between it and other residential areas in Rome were invisible to him. She asked him how long they would have to walk around before he kissed her. He hadn't thought about it, but was pleased that she had.

I like this memory; it's one of the few times Jelena was explicit in wanting affection from me.

They walked some more, holding hands, looking for a pizza place she knew, but it was closed for the afternoon, and they kissed once more, then decided to drop his bags off before they headed for her new park.

They rode through Rome, he was exhilarated to see it all again. He tried to tell her how beautiful it all was, but his banal comments were lost in the rushing wind. As they went along she sang a folk song loudly and tunefully.

They reached her apartment, which was outside the centre, though not far out by London standards. It was in a large anonymous block next to the covered market where she bought her fruit and drank her coffee each morning. The area was attractive even though it lacked distinction. It was close to the Tiber, and had none of the mordancy which marked the residential districts of his own city. She gave him some keys which would be useful for bad times, and he hulked his bag into the little lift in which they ascended to the ninth floor. It was a space filled with memories of their old battles, where they had been so angry that they had both tried to shove out the door at the same time, and in one fracas he remembered he had lost a button from his favourite shirt. He had lost that shirt as well, now. They were calm this time, attracted to each other, not saying much.

She shared the flat with about six people and a couple of dogs, but it didn't seem as overcrowded as that. No one was home, or at least not visibly or audibly. She asked him whether he was hungry (her mother had told her that hunger caused his bad temper, a theory also shared by his mother). He truthfully answered that he was. She had bought for his visit: courgettes, prosciutto, mortadella, pizza bianco, and tomatoes. He sat down at the laminated table and watched as she began frying diced courgettes on the camping stove which occupied most of the counter. She assembled all the food on the table in front of him. He ate a couple of pieces of pizza, but she got angry that he was leaving no room for the large amount of pasta and sauce that she was cooking, so he stopped. He offered his help with the cooking, but she refused it. There was not much else to talk about.

Soon it was ready. He ate a lot of spaghetti with sauce and a heavy grating of parmesan. She ate a little pasta and some whole courgettes that she had boiled in the pot with the spaghetti. The open windows of the small kitchen had a view of the market from high above, other apartment blocks, and in the distance green hills. Afterwards he felt quite full; they had eaten fast and quietly. Jelena and Water went to her bedroom. They sat together on her single bed. He began to kiss her, shadowing sex. She wanted to drink champagne first, so he retrieved it from the fridge. It was still warm. He drew the wooden blind, darkening the room, and she locked the door. They undressed, Adam and Eve in a small room with an *en suite* bathroom in a shared apartment in the north of Rome. Twice they fucked, quickly and hoping it would make them close again. Because it was necessary, they wanted to.

What is there to say about sex? It merges with all the other forgotten things we are obsessed with. Only a few occasions stick in the head, and that's usually because of context.

After they had showered, it felt like the beginning had been concluded. He said he would like to go to the new park she liked, but it was too late in the afternoon and the weather was not fine, so they went to see a film instead, and then were tired, falling asleep quickly in her small hot room.

3

More description. No man is an island. No man's land.

The hydrofoil to Procida had no deck. The cloistered passengers were indifferent to the retreating views of Naples, drawing the thick curtains on the daylight voyage, perhaps to fix their vision on the interior of the unsteady craft or maybe, as Jelena remarked on his mentioning this, because constantly surrounded by such beauty they no longer cared for it. It was an hour's journey before you saw 'Cinema Procida' in very large letters written on a medium-sized building. The boat, like an airplane waiting for a landing slot, was for some reason forced to wait outside the harbour. No traffic was visible in the blue sea. The port or town stretching for an unknown distance inland and along the coast was quiet because it was Monday. Her friend had told them that there were pretty places away from the new port. She walked quickly out of the port uphill on what seemed to be the main road. It was lined with largish houses and the occasional business; he was tired, carrying her not too heavy bag and his small rucksack in the afternoon sunshine, but not grumpy as he often was in similar situations. Still, he didn't feel like making any decisions.

They came to a square with a tobacconist, a few shops and some public telephones. She used one of them to phone a number her friend had given her, but that place was full. They sat on the shaded concrete benches in the square. Some boys packed things onto their motorbikes and then drove off. She went to the tobacconist to ask if anyone knew somewhere to stay. The young man who worked there had something nearby he was willing to rent them. They followed him round the corner to see a pleasant two-floored apartment at a reasonable price. Neither of them knew where they were or how far the sea was. The man said it was about ten minutes' walk but you never knew how long that was, so they said they needed to think about it. He explained to them which bus to take to where they had been told was most beautiful. They bought two tickets and waited for the bus. One came but it was the wrong number. They argued. She took her bag and walked off down a walled path. He followed her. She ran away from him and he did not follow her. He turned to walk down to the port where they had arrived. She was angry and hated him. He had had enough of her.

At the port he ate a large ice cream, with cream on top of the ice cream. He then looked at a timetable for the boats to Naples.

He bought a ticket for the ferry which was departing in half an hour. He had in his bag the key to her flat in Rome; he could get there by train late that night, sleep there, go to the airport in the morning and fly home. Waiting for the boat he didn't think much, only that this was final, but he had thought that before. The ferry arrived and lowered its large metal flap to let passengers on; Water waited a while for the crowds to be swallowed up by the boat, then walked on and up the metal stairs to the lower deck. For a short time he stood there. There he made up his mind, pushed his way back down the stairs past some stragglers just boarding, and was off the boat. A few seconds later thick chains began raising the ferry's heavy door as it glided away from the dock on the calm sea. He found a payphone to call her. She answered that she was just arriving back at the port. He sat down on a stone bollard in the sunshine looking out to sea, and he also had a view of the traffic entering by the main road which they had climbed earlier. She arrived on the back of a motorbike belonging to a hotelier, whose hotel they were not going to be staying in. Someone else had called back to say there was room for them. This time Water told her they would take a taxi. They climbed into the car and drove back up the hill, uncomfortable near each other.

He woke still angry with her. It was another completely clear sunny day, and she had been awake and gone to the hospital already. The previous night he had laughed at her for being a hypochondriac about her slightly swollen hand, but by morning her knuckles were no longer visible. The doctors could not decide whether it was blood poisoning or an allergic reaction, so she had to have twice daily injections and also take pills. She returned from the hospital with some fruit and Diet Coke for herself and no bread for him. She began to clean, telling him he was dirty and disgusting, and what he must do, and that he was doing it wrong, what was wrong with him. He showered and left, telling her to go fuck herself, stupid bitch.

They stayed in a self-contained portion of a large bungalow. It was a pretty house surrounded by a walled garden filled with lemon trees (the most noticable flora on the island, whose giant fruit were a source of local pride). Their part of the house was dark and private enough to almost feel alone in. The old woman, who owned the main house had at first been friendlier to him, but she soon realized he spoke little Italian, and then came round mainly when he was out. She always wore the same striped man's shirt and loose tan trousers held up with a thick black leather belt. Water had to restrain himself from staring at her large hands with their dirty nails matching those of her sandaled toes. It was difficult for him to determine whether he disliked her. She was always coming over for a cigarette or some bread, or to see how Jelena's hand was. He got sick of her, but Jelena liked her and kept offering her more stuff, guiltily giving her a steak Water had grilled, or a fish they didn't want to cook.

The island was small and sunny enough to make him aware of the sun's position in the sky and its relation to north, south, east and west. He fancied that this was the way the early sailors had felt, surrounded by sea, yet ready to head out reassured by knowing that the rise and fall of the sun would always tell them where they were. He walked south. Most of Procida's circumference was steep, eroding rock. There were many paths going off from the roads to tempt bold travellers on hot days, but they led only to dead ends, private property signs or more houses. It seemed like there were no shortcuts and no way out except from the port, or by private boat from one of the other harbours, yet he did not feel a sense of claustrophobia; either the heat or his anger had liberated him from his holidaymaker unease.

He walked fast under the high sun, thinking that he should keep the sun on his left, knowing that it was unnecessary to care where the sun was as this was the only road he could take and it was even almost straight. The harbour he arrived in, after only fifteen minutes' walk, was at the southern end of the island. Such a pleasure to go from centre to end so quickly. At the harbour were yesterday's memories of sitting eating a pizza, watching the occasional boat arrive bringing its sailors of leisure, rich families on holiday probably. He and Jelena had sat with their feet over the water, flurries of fish ignoring all, he throwing pebbles into the sea, she up and down to find out if their pizza was ready. She hated him. They had a Napolitana and she told him that they had joked in the pizzeria that they called it a Roma on the island, as they were too close to Naples to use it as a name.

He turned uphill from the harbour, the way he hadn't been before. Disappointingly there were only glimpses of the sea on another narrow road on which every passing car forced you to flatten yourself against the flanking walls. There were no cliff paths on Procida; either they had fallen into the sea, or it was too difficult to build them, or no one cared to. Maybe they just didn't need them, nor tourists either. Soon he was round one quarter of Procida at the beach where he had found Jelena before. She had been there asleep on the brown sand. They had quarrelled again before sunset. Now he scanned the beach for her bright towel, and walked along the sand, but could not find her. He was hot, but he resisted the urge to swim and kept on walking. Upstairs into the higher town, then downstairs into another sheltered harbour, where they had eaten on their first night on the island. The cats were there, hanging around, waiting for scraps. Up and down again, and he was back where they had arrived at the port, from south to north.

He walked slowly up the road from the port to their house, past the archway of trellised flowers framing the sea, and a bar which was much less glamorous than it should have been. Past the shops of which he had already chosen a couple to be his, the church, the drunk with his fat stomach too big for his dirty shorts, the general store with its TV and stuff for the beach. He stopped at the one payphone which he knew worked, and called her. She was at the beach near the south harbour. He took a bus, which came quickly, and was there in less than ten minutes. He was sick of walking.

She was reading a book she'd never finish. He joked that he had run there to be there so quickly. She wasn't amused; he was annoyed that she didn't care. She responded nastily to everything he said. He dug a hole in the sand with his hands, disappointed by the odd piece of jagged glass or cigarette butt he found. He formed the sand into a person with a screaming gothic face and stones for eyes. She went for a swim and he watched for her, looking into the setting sun which made her disappear into the glinting sea. It was stupid for him to be unhappy when all was so beautiful and they were young and healthy. But she hated him. And he wasn't thinking hard enough to figure out why. She hated him, and he was silent at last.

On the boat home she put on her sunglasses and ignored his fidgety presence. He went to buy an ice cream, then a can of Coke then a Mars bar. She didn't want anything, and he felt slightly queasy from too much sugar. He wanted the energy to think. It might be too late when they got off the boat in Naples. He felt time drain away. It had to be decided. The good aesthetics of making a choice while at sea would be lost if not. On dry land it would be real and firm and over. So he thought, trying to explore all the angles. He stared at her angry figure sitting pressed against the railing as if she were trying to slide into the rushing sea. Then they saw Naples. And they disembarked and he had lost his chance because there was not enough time, or he had lacked courage.

So I had decided to ask her to marry me, because I wanted to. But she was always angry at me, so I didn't. This was all before I met Harriet. Before I married Harriet, which was before I married Jelena.

4

Another descriptive chapter. It's easier to get into a book if it doesn't start off too fancy. Me and Jelena together – what no one can understand, though I promised they would if they read my novel. I got engaged to Jelena, then split up with her, got married to Harriet, got divorced from her, then got married to Jelena. Got it? This is before Harriet still.

Bratislava is the capital city of Slovakia. It had been the capital of somewhere more important for a while, and not really a capital of anywhere for long periods, just a town on a European river. Now it was building itself again: the historic centre was being spruced up for the tourists, and modern asymmetric office blocks of glass and concrete were springing up to hold the management consultants and accountants sent to advise the natives, former communists, how to make a profit from their Pizza Hut franchises.

Water wondered whether it wouldn't be cheaper for people just to read some books on business and good capitalism rather than pay these recent graduates from Europe and America's best business schools. Jelena told him that NATO and the European Union had forced Slovakia to accept all this junk: fast food, supermarkets and the sale of their industries to multinationals. It was one of the conditions for considering letting them join the rich countries' club. A pity. Sad being a tourist these days. Everywhere you went the same old stuff. But at least the ubiquitous Magnum was a third of the London price. If he wanted to, Water could eat oysters and fillet steak and drink martinis, every meal every day in all the best restaurants of Bratislava, and lick twenty Magnums a day, and drink magnums of the local pretend champagne, and eat three cakes and drink three coffees with cognac, when he wanted to. He could have done the same thing in London, but it was a lot cheaper in Slovakia. Actually, he preferred to eat with Jelena's parents in their house and only ate out when he was by himself, having quarrelled with her.

The circus never stopped, and the depths they plunged to seemed limitless. The boundaries of what they could say or do to each other were never set, but when they were apart for a little while they realized that they liked each other, and this became proof of their love, so Water asked Jelena to marry him. Marriage to a person you hated, feared, tormented and blamed seemed romantic to them, to him. It freed marriage from its conformity and convention, made it noble again. What's the use of anything? Only useless things are worth doing. So Water thought.

A slice of cake filled with marzipan for him, and one with cream for her. Two coffees. Four o'clock in the main square in Bratislava, catching sight of the same people you had noticed an hour before in one of the small city's other streets. So unlike London, where a beautiful face glimpsed would be lost in the millions, never to be viewed again. Their waitress was nowhere to be seen, so he could not get the bill. Jelena and Water sat silently together in the Café Refute. He preferred to read his book than talk to her. All she said was stupid and annoyed him. He wanted to correct her all the time, to teach her how to be. Though if she did try to do what he wanted he was embarrassed, so hated her. Instead she made nearly every moment miserable and difficult, from waking him up early and shouting at him to pushing him away when he tried to kiss her at night. If he allowed himself any self-satisfaction, to be pleased for one second with one of his little achievements, she would point it out and prick his bubble, making him feel foolish and angry again. He admired her resistance.

They had separate bedrooms in her parents' house. He didn't know what they thought or even knew. Her father and mother spoke no English. He had learned only a few words of their language, could say 'please', 'thank you' and 'good'. He enjoyed the novelty of being polite and appreciative. He made sure to keep his mouth shut when he ate, and not to clink his spoon on the soup bowl, and even tried to stay standing until her parents had sat down for dinner, but that proved impractical and showy. In return Jelena ate with her fingers, burped and complained about her mother's cooking. The four of them sat in the bright room with its view of the trees, which Water had seen in winter and summer now. Jelena's parents were prosperous, both nearly retired, her mother an architect who had designed the house, her father a professor of law. The house was simple and clean, only details seemed foreign to him. The unpainted wooden door frames and skirting, on the walls some paintings reminiscent of Malevich, a couple of traditional jugs and vases, the decorations at Christmas and Easter. The air was drier. People admired trees more than flowers, and big dogs barked from large wire-fenced gardens.

Her mother placed the two largest schnitzels on his plate and asked him whether he would like more French fries. Water liked the honour of the big portions, the attention paid to him as the hungry man, the guest and prospective son-in-law. Jelena told him that she and her father hated her mother's schnitzels and that her mother was happy when he came because it gave her the chance to cook them. Water did not question the assumptions behind the familial logic. He ate too much of the battered pork fried in pork fat, accompanied by pickled hot peppers, French fries and tomato and cucumber salad with basil from the garden. They had started with soup.

My favourite thing is to remember food. The obsession is strong; it punctuates our days, the hunger which is never real.

Jelena's father sat next to Water. They were too close to each other for comfort. Her father always left the table as soon as he finished eating. Jelena, her mother and Water remained for pudding, chocolates and conversation interpreted sporadically by Jelena. It all made Water ready for sleep. It was a nightly play, which was as unreal for her parents as it was for Water and Jelena, but nevertheless a performance they all seemed to enjoy. Jelena said it was tiring acting as the go-between, but she too appreciated the dinnertime respite from being at war and in love with Water. Her father often returned to chase their houndish dog out into the hall with a stick that Water had found during a walk in the woods. The dog, called Gordon, would soon return and Jelena would then encourage it onto the upholstered sofa to the faux-horror of her mother.

They walked back through the woods with her dog on his extendable leash. It was not safe to let Gordon run free. Once when he had been let loose he had been hit by a car, though not seriously injured. A child rode by on a tricycle, a young man shouted to his friends, there were dog walkers and runners. The woods were busy. There was even a log cabin café at its centre serving drinks and meals to hale folk.

'Don't talk to me. I can't hear you any more,' Water said, putting his finger in his ears.

She tried to punch him, but he dodged out of the way.

'You're a grumpy shit. I am not going to listen to you moan anymore,' he said.

She laughed. It was funny for a moment, Water, fingers in ears, insulting her.

Water kissed her.

'You are a shit,' she said, and slapped him on the back of the head. He hit her back.

'Why can't you stop yourself? You never have any restraint,' said Water.

'You a sadist. Psychopath. You hit me. Why did you hit me?'

Because we speak different languages all conversations must include many synonyms and repetitions to make sure the correct meaning is conveyed.

He walked away from her quickly. The dog in the woods looked like he was in a hunting painting. Water couldn't just walk off. Only finally and forever back to England, which was a long way away. Because they were staying with her parents they were stuck together. He slowed down.

'What's your mother making for dinner tonight?' he asked.

'You should marry my darling mother. You love each other so much. Mamicka, Waterko. You would be happy.'

'At least she doesn't make me miserable all the time. I don't know if I'd want to fuck her though.'

'You don't even know how to do that. You grumpy shit,' she said.

'I am going to beat you with a stick if you don't shut up.' In the woods a man said this to a woman with a dog.

When they got back to her house he said hello to her mother and went to take a shower. His room was in the studio section of the house. He had his own bathroom. The windows of the house were triple glazed, and covered by both shutters and curtains. The walls were solid, so it was a good place to sleep undisturbed long after everyone else had woken. Only Jelena ever woke him up early.

That night an actress and her husband came to dinner. Jelena's parents knew many of the people you saw on Slovakian TV, from the newsreaders to the politicians, even the stars of old movies. They would be identified as one of the old men or women you had met in the street the day before. The actress had bouffant mahogany hair and expressive lips and hands. Her husband looked like a politician. His clothes were too formal for the occasion. They brought their daughter, a childhood friend of Jelena's, whose tragic temperament was visible in her long thick hair, but contradicted by her everyday pretty face. Once Water had been introduced as the guest from Great Britain his part was over and the conversation touched on him infrequently. It was boring pretending to pay attention, watching their mouths move. He moved to the kitchen where Jelena was preparing a pasta dish she had learned to make in Rome.

The actress's daughter soon joined them to show them some photos of her recent Italian holiday with her American boyfriend. She spoke good English, of course. That was them on the beach, them in Pompeii, them camping. Her boyfriend looked adolescent and Water realised he himself was still not old, hiding from the grown-ups in the kitchen. They were ugly photos of beautiful places. And Jelena's old friend with her American boyfriend, who had cried when her mother had sung an old folk song, was ridiculous, and Water never wanted to be boring, though he didn't mind being bored. And Jelena's friend, whose arm Jelena had broken when they were little, had nearly been killed once, had escaped death at the hands of a murderer, Jelena said, which didn't sound real.

After dinner everyone begged the actress to sing. She protested, clasping her hands to her chest. Then she sang for a long time with a powerful voice, her eyes and her *r*s rolling. Water imagined that the crystal vase on the heavy dresser might shatter as she hit the high notes. Then the dog began to howl in duet, which brought the recital to an end with everyone laughing. The actress, her husband and her daughter then went home laughing. Water told them to visit him if they were ever in London.

After eight days Jelena's father drove him to the station. Water would take twenty hours by train to reach his home. It would give him time to think about what he had not done. It had never been the right time to tell, ask her parents when he had spent all day telling their daughter to fuck off. Why had he come if that wasn't what he was going to do. It was embarrassing, but still it was wrong to announce your intent to marry just because it seemed appropriate. Either way it was a mess. He had lost his credibility with her parents, and thus with Jelena to an extent. He had gone from suitor to joker. He believed he had done the right thing in stretching Jelena's faith further. If marriage meant much, it meant nothing. At the station Jelena waited with him. An ugly couple kissed next to them, the woman's hand on the man's ass. A pair of happy young couples rushed laughing onto the platform. Water said goodbye to Jelena, and tried to kiss her on the lips, but she turned away and he boarded the train home.

5

Another way to begin would be to tell you about my family. First Father. Father, Mother and the Holy Ghost. My father annoys me and I annoy him . In a sentimental way we love each other. I cannot separate myself from my criticisms of him, because they apply to me too.

When Water was fifteen he went to visit his father in America.

America's a big country I always say, full of different types of people, individuals. Not these generic Americans we (us, all the same English) like to believe here in England.

They hadn't seen each other for a while. Water's father was living in a small university town in New England. His father's town had pubs brewing their own organic beers, average Italian restaurants serving American-Italian food, craft shops smelling of incense, ice cream parlours selling heavy ice cream full of bits and pieces and pizza delivery: all the usual amenities. By its lake, which froze solid enough in winter for cars to drive across it, were cycle, rollerblade, or cross-country ski paths. The town was full of students living together in large or small houses, driving their cars and drinking illegally. It was a pleasant town that you could not hate unless you lived there. It was where Water had been born and lived for his first four years. He took from it a taste for beef jerky and an indifference to cold.

Meat sticks are what I mean by beef jerky, Slim Jims they're called, and they're spicy enough to make you sneeze, made from recovered beef I imagine, which means they hose grim bits of flesh from the dead cow's bones, then grind it up, add some flavour enhancers, form it into cylinders and sell them to kids.

Water's father picked him up from the airport. The heater was on in the car because the temperature was below zero. Although snow hadn't fallen for a while it lay grey on the ground and in big piles ploughed up. Sat low in the seat of his father's Japanese car (a Toyota), Water looked for meaning in the landscape, tried to suck some emotion out of what he saw through the window.

'What do you think, Nat?' his father asked, using his silly old name.

'It's all right.'

They drove through the poor area of his father's town. A few black people lived there, as well as a noticeable number of obese people. The rest of the town was white. A lack of diversity which embarrassed the town's liberal citizens.

His father's place was downtown near the department, where he was called 'Professor Water'.

This status title embarrasses me when I repeat it.

His girlfriend of that time lived with him, and for extra income they rented out the ground floor of their large wooden house to students. Professor Water's girlfriend was a fattish woman with long gray hair in a ponytail, whose attraction the fifteen-year-old Water could not comprehend. She, Sarah, was younger than his father, but Water understood why she liked him. He was Water's father, after all.

Old people fucking?

Sarah tried to welcome him warmly but Water took an instant dislike to her. Her hair is greasy and she smells of onions, he thought. When he was older he would look upon that visit with a mixture of shame and pride in his childish cruelty.

Water made his father take them to an all-you-can-eat seafood restaurant. His mother had recommended it, telling him he would enjoy the fried clams there (although her last visit had been ten years before, and she was allergic to fish).

'We'll go wherever Nat wants to,' Sarah had insisted when his father tried to suggest another restaurant.

The Sailor by the Shore had red-and-white check tablecloths, cocktails served from the wooden bar, fishing nets hanging from the ceiling, wheels and barometers fixed to the walls and a terrace overlooking the lake.

They had horrible little rolls and butter, and funny tubs of coleslaw. 'Want a beer?' asked his father.

'No thanks,' replied Water.

A couple, old friends of the family, came up to say hello. The man's wife had been his babysitter. Water didn't remember her.

The fried shrimp or the fried oysters gave Sarah and Water's father diarrhoea, for which they threatened to sue the restaurant, and were subsequently compensated with $1,400 each.

Water, in a sulky way, enjoyed those two weeks with his father. They went to discount clothing stores where Water pored over racks of shirts and trousers looking for items reduced from $300 to $40. They drove round town looking for places Water might remember. Water liked the university library. He took out many volumes of philosophy and read them rather than make conversation with Sarah. When she spoke he contradicted her. When she cooked he was not hungry. When she was interested he sneered. Sarah was not a nice woman and Water was nasty to her.

We left America on a boat. This is one of the only childhood memories I have. But the way I have written it has merged two boat memories into one anecdote.

When Water was four his whole family had left America for England on a boat. His mother had grown tired of the neighbours. She was tired of his father as well but hoped that things might be better in London. On the boat Water insisted, despite his mother's warnings, on purchasing a penknife and opening the blade. Having cut himself, he watched the red blood ooze out of the thin slit in his finger, and fainted for the first time in his life. The boat was good for children. It was exciting to be sailing across the Atlantic, and only scary when you looked over through the rope railings and saw the grey deep ocean ready to take you in. For the rest of his life Water always dreamt of that ocean. If they had not travelled to London Water might never have painted so much.

'Nat, you'd make a good lawyer,' his father said, now their time together was at an end. No more battles to be won, the combatants could acknowledge each other's strengths. One night Sarah had left the house crying because she could stand Water and/or his father no longer.

'You're more facetious than your Uncle Joey or your mother,' said Water's father.

'By facetious you mean I don't agree with you. You would know anyway, you're the most facetious person I've ever met.'

'I learned it from you,' replied his father.

Water's mother and sisters had taught him that physical affection, hugs and kisses between siblings and parents, were sentimental. One of his friends once came for New Year at his house in London and told Water that his family was the first totally ironic family he had ever met.

Everyone says irony is for idealists.

His father hugged him goodbye at the airport. Water stiffly reciprocated. From the air the little town where he was born, a small city really, was a brown and white pattern.

His father split with Sarah, they sued each other, and he replaced her in his photo frames with someone else.

6

Mother. My mother. Mother fucker. No I don't have an Oedipus complex. Yuck. I love my mother. Yucker. Fuck her.

His mother had a talent for psychology, for infiltrating her children's thoughts and making them behave as she thought best. They generally fulfilled her ambitions, because they wanted her to love them, and because she merely filled their world with her ideas rather than proscribing or prohibiting.

When she was younger his mother had painted pictures and written for magazines. She had known important people and tried her hand at many jobs. Whatever she did she could not achieve success. Of course it was more difficult for women then, but her problem was her refusal to accept the world as it was, she preferred her ideals and superstitious morality, do unto others as you would have them do unto you, which Water thought involved an irrational fear that if you did something bad it would happen to you too. Her children, old people, sick dogs, occupied most of her energies. Her intelligence found many ways to justify her lack of fulfilment.

During one summer of his childhood Water's mother fell ill with bronchitis from smoking cigarettes, or perhaps the imminent divorce from his father. His sisters and father were not there. Sometimes they were, but Water remembered that he had been alone with his mother. The woods behind his house, where he walked the dogs every evening, were densely leaved, making them seem bigger than they were. The dogs, which had been nominally acquired and owned by various members of the family, were so badly behaved that they could not be trusted not to bite someone or run off, so it was better to walk them when the woods were empty.

Water liked the quiet repetition of his walk in the woods. His family lived on a street, called a 'gardens', which was a dead end, terminating at a tube station. Every evening their neighbour Weiss, who had survived the Holocaust, would go to buy the *Standard* at the underground kiosk. Every evening you could see him shuffling back along the street in his brown mackintosh with his newspaper in his hand. When Mr Weiss died his wife gave them some of his stuff which she didn't want around anymore. Water got his watch, two leather wallets and some wooden boxes. A couple of brown raincoats hung in his family's closets until they were finally thrown away, their lining eaten by moths.

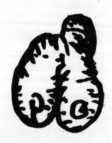

We lived in Highgate. A nice-ish rich place. Weiss was old, short, with brown skin (I mean tanned-looking white skin).

That summer Water painted a portrait of his poorly mother in her dressing gown sitting up in bed. His mother could not bring herself to look at it afterwards because she found it so depressing. He also painted a realistic picture of his stupid dog which was the best he'd done, and that was when Water knew he could paint anything. He painted a picture of a swimming pool, and the colours he chose looked good together. He did a cubist painting too.

I really painted these pictures. You can see them one day. My mother's got the swimming pool one in a frame.

Water probably made his mother scrambled eggs three times at most, but in his mind he had cooked them for her every day that summer. She told him how to do it properly. Slowly. First you melted the butter, then stirred the eggs over a low heat which tried your patience, and your reward was light and good scrambled eggs to be served on buttered toast with bacon and fried tomatoes. A humidifier steamed all the time in his mother's bedroom while she wheezed and coughed up phlegm. From her window the garden seemed merged with the thick woods. The wallpaper slid from the damp walls.

His mother got better. Water's parents split up. The dogs behaved worse on their walks.

For a while his mother went most days to help the Buchwalds, an old couple who once, years ago in another country and culture, had been art historians or anthropologists. One of his sisters accompanied his mother, returning with interesting old books in German, and they always talked about Mrs Buchwald's wit or

Mr Buchwald's illness. Water was dimly aware that the Buchwalds were the geriatric pair he saw walking by very slowly, too slowly to get anywhere. He did not even know which house they lived in. They died, one at a time, and from their things Water was given a little box with a fine veneered inlay.

Death of neighbours, my mother ill, the first memory of caring for someone treasured by me as a souvenir of pleasurable altruism.

7

The prodigy. I am so in love with myself that I can't see how good I am. As a child I was conscious that it might all be written down one day. If I hadn't become famous my life would have gone in the slag heap of megalomaniacal hopes with all the other crap people who have swallowed too many self-improvement manuals. What a terrible sentence.

(Water had always been good at drawing and painting since he was a child. He had four sisters and no brothers. He was the youngest, like Picasso and Einstein. His mother told him he had no imagination, which was true, but you didn't need it to be a good painter, you just needed to be good at painting. Other middle-class children visited Monet shows, but Water's mother didn't care to force-feed him culture. He preferred computer games and television like most stupid kids.)

That's why.

Anyway, they had run out of money and his father had returned to America. His sisters were all most talented and had gone off to good universities, so Water spent a lot of time by himself, relieving his boredom by painting still-lifes and masturbating. At thirteen, combining his interests, he moved onto drawing classes where he drew the sagging flesh of the life models. At fifteen his mother forced an art school to accept him too early and he entered the art world. He didn't like paintings, but he liked painting.

From foundation, to Oxford, to the Royal College of Art in Kensington Gore.

Glittering prizes. Crappy places. I did go to these institutions. And they were OK sometimes. Oxford was disappointing: boring mediocre sexless students planning to become management consultants or lawyers. Bad food too.

His first interview at the Royal College was not a success. 'Why do you need to come to the Royal College of Art when you are so certain about your work? What do you want to learn here?' Water hadn't the right answers; he didn't realize he had too many answers for an eighteen-year-old; the tutors, mostly veterans, preferred neediness to confidence, better confusion than too much purpose.

The next year he was cannier. 'I have a lot to learn. I'd like to talk to and learn from other artists. This would be an incredible opportunity. My paintings are about my family history and

television's banality. They are less certain than they used to be.'
He got in.

It's good to get in. I felt great when I got the acceptance letter. Same with Oxford.

On his first day he carried a bright orange bag, which he thought made him look less threatening. He made friends with everyone: the popular, the strange, the older students and the foreign ones. He was always ready to help or listen, and flattered the prettier girls without offending those that were not. He kept in mind his father's dictum: start with the ugly girls and work your way up. He painted as well, but never boasted anymore of his genius.

Would that this next bit were true. I did make a lot of friends but managed to offend most of the tutors by being arrogant (people's favourite word to describe me) and a trouble-maker, and screwed up on making the right contacts with the visiting artists.

He became friends with the visiting artists who came to lecture. He knew that being attentive would take him further than impressing with his cleverness. The young and successful artists had influence with the galleries he wanted. 'Yes John, I love skiing. You should come with me and my friends, we've got this place free. You know these rich kids.' So the better artists drank with him, holidayed with him, and liked him.

In January the painting students took a trip to Madrid. Madrid had no water. Other great cities had big rivers or the sea, but Madrid was dry and inland, marooned in the centre of Spain. There were many shops with hanging hams, and you noticed the absence of Jews and Muslims. You could stay up all night in Madrid. But the city was really all about the Prado.

I sound like a third-rate travel guide for people who think they're sophisticated. I don't want to describe anything, but then how will you know where I was? Read a good book about Madrid. Or better, go there yourself.

Water liked Madrid immediately. Firstly he had never been there before, secondly on his first night a couple of women shouted 'beautiful' at him. Like most people, Water could never resist being liked. That evening the students of the Royal College wandered the streets, going out at 7pm, seven hours too early, and found bars, discos, gunpoint muggings, Chinese restaurants and Irish pubs. In their drunken, out-of-school daze, nothing impinged on their happiness.

The next day most of them assembled, hungover, at the Prado. Water expected to be bored by more old paintings. He wandered around with Mark, one of the few friends with whom he felt he could share his cynicism.

Mark's a web designer now.

They laughed at the silliness of painters, forced to paint religious or mythological subjects, and to make every brush mark painstakingly invisible, hoping for the patronage of an enlightened despot. Walking past masterpiece after masterpiece, he and Mark pretended to be dumb American tourists, literally ignoring everything but the peculiar.

Mark and Water went into a low-lit room filled with only two other tourists and five greyish paintings by Goya. The paintings from the house of the deaf man, painted by Goya on the walls of his house before he died and after he was deaf and had finished thrilling and flattering royalty with his softly focused portraits. Eighty-two when he died in 1828. The paintings in that room showed a giant eating a woman, two giants beating each other, a dog howling alone, three magi together floating above a landscape while a soldier takes aim, a crowd of refugees in cinemascope, a devil playing his guitar to a mass of people round a campfire. They were not boring. Water couldn't not look at them. Maybe he was still drunk, but they wouldn't let him go. They were the first paintings Water had seen that were as moving as movies.

I used this gumpf on a statement applying for a Rome scholarship, which I got. Forgive me if it sounds toothily sincere.

That afternoon Water and Mark shouted about Goya's room to their friends. 'That's what paintings should be like. They're great. Even a cretin would like them. They set the standard: we should do even better.' Water forgot his pretend modesty in his excitement.

After that Water got a lot of ham from one of the shops filled with counters, mirrors and hundreds of hams, smelling of leather, and ate enough to feel sick. He then consumed an entire can of anchovy-stuffed olives. Then Water sat at a café near the Ritz drinking a piña colada, looking out at the busy traffic passing a grand monument. Then, then, then, then, then, then.

In London, having sold a lot of paintings at his final college show and excited a few galleries who could wait, he decided to go to Rome for a year before he became famous.

His girlfriend of the time was a little saddened by his departure. Water made sure to break up with her before he left, so he wouldn't be distracted while in Rome.

I have converted the whole brilliant spectacle of my life into a lot of tame, self-aggrandising anecdotes.

8

Even love can be eviscerated by words. From before I went to Rome.

'I love you,' said Water.

The tall pretty woman did not reply; she just tilted her head to one side.

'I love you, do you understand? I don't love many people, only one before. I love you.'

'You don't really love me, Nathaniel. I am going back soon so it's easy to say you love me,' she answered, smiling.

'I am Water. Not Nathaniel, Nat or anything else. Call me by my name: Water.'

This speech was one of Nathaniel Water's favourites, showing off his attractive firmness of identity. He tried to kiss her on the lips but she turned her head away.

'You know I cannot,' said Ariane. She looked beautiful now. Face flushed, unruly brown hair and blue eyes, where a little sadness showed. She was ten years older than Water.

'Do what you want,' said Water, and took her hand in his, his hand holding her fingers. She did not pull away.

They walked through Regent's Park up past the little lake at 6pm when the park was nearly empty as the sky turned blue-red. If you had seen them you would have thought they were in love. Water knew Ariane was right, in a way; she was leaving, and so he did not have to imagine spending years being her boyfriend. She had a boyfriend, anyway, whom Water never thought about.

They had been at a party most of the previous night, which Water had organized to say goodbye to Ariane. They danced and got drunk with their friends and Water had thought they might have sex that night but he had been too tired to convince her.

Now as they walked, he felt an electric attraction between them and wanted to touch her.

'Electric attraction' sounds rubbish. But you do sometimes feel it. It feels good.

'I love you,' he tried again.

One night in heavy rain outside Paddington Station, as he walked her home from a bar, he had told her he loved her for the first time. Earlier they had had a running race, for which the winner took their choice of prize from the loser. Before the race she would sometimes playfully hit him when they argued, so he knew she liked him. He chose a kiss as his prize. He cried, maybe because the wind was hurting his eyes, and told her he loved her, and he remembered, but was not sure, that she had told him she loved him too.

I am so smugly happy with myself. With my crappy memories of my brilliant posturing. I am sure these events must have had some real meaning besides my triumph of eventual indifference. I can't face really remembering; that would require too much effort to go back. I refuse.

They were through the park now and he went to hug her, but she would not respond, thinking of her return to her boyfriend and not wanting to have too much to forget.

Walk through Regent's Park at sunset and look at all the silly happy couples. Remember me and Ariane. Or buy an ice cream cone, though actually you probably won't find somewhere open at that time of day.

They wrote to each other after she went back. Letters that were not ardent but hinted at great love. Her letters were intelligent in their imperfect English. They made him feel he must be in love with her, a state that he felt necessitated bold action.

Beware: bad English makes foreign people sound more profound.

A month after her departure he flew to see her in Vienna. An old friend of his lived there, so he didn't tell Ariane he was coming. Water had no plan, but was interested to know what would happen. He wanted to know why for the first time in his life he had not been able to sleep well.

I have spent so much of life asleep, dreaming forgotten dreams. It seems a waste. Occasional insomnia is therefore a blessing.

The weekend he arrived Ariane was in the country staying at her boyfriend's parents. Water, who liked all cities, liked Vienna. It was bourgeois but its atmosphere hinted at a Central European life, a cultural alternative. Tourists did not command the usual servility. In a wood-panelled café near the centre, standing up, he ate open sandwiches of savoury combinations, chosen from a glass case. The place had no windows. Off the main street a kneeling

Jew, cast in bronze, wearing a barbed wire crown, washed the pavement.

Details of holidays I have been on. Food I ate, a few buildings and things I noticed. Blah, blah, but you need to set the scene, don't you. There are some good paintings in every European capital.

On Monday Ariane was back. When his friends asked him why he went to Vienna he told them, 'I went for love'. That Monday he never mentioned love to Ariane. They drove around Vienna with a mutual friend, and in the evening they went to a party. Seeing her again he could not be sure what he felt and therefore what to say. He wanted to know, but he sensed many things and could not read her mind. He did not touch her except for a polite embrace hello and a kiss goodbye.

On Tuesday she held a dinner party where for the first time he met her boyfriend. Water tried to be light-hearted and intelligent, but only managed to get drunk without seeming terribly drunk. Her boyfriend Moritz was scholarly. A serious normal person of her own age. Water did not hate him, nor conceive that he could be his rival.

On his last night, Ariane and Water went to dinner without anyone else, in a restaurant that served something besides schniztel or goulash, but nothing much better. It was designed for successful professionals and so could be described as nondescript. He sat opposite her in a padded chair.

'I came here to see you.'

'You wanted a romantic holiday,' she replied.

'I don't know what you mean in your letters. Do you still like me? I wanted to talk to you, and we spend all our time with friends,' said Water.

'What should I do? What can I do?' Her emotion scared him

and he did not have an answer for her, nor did he want to make any promises that he would have to keep.

'You like Moritz more than me, more than you like me?'

'Moritz is important. We have been together for seven years. I don't like to talk about him with you.'

'I am good,' said Water, as though that were enough.

That was as far as they got. She took him back and they sat together in the car, outside his friend's house, not kissing for a long time. Water didn't know what she wanted or what he could offer.

That is what happened. It is important enough to record, for we must keep these love memories. They are to be preserved for a while and then go in the bin with some old Christmas cards when we die.

A few years later Water visited Vienna for an important show. Again they were together in a bar with friends. Ariane and Moritz's six-month-old son was at home with his father. Water thought, as he looked at Ariane, 'I love you'. They shared a taxi home, Water's friend slammed the door shut between them as they said goodbye and the taxi drove off.

French movie poignancy.

9

Another girlfriend from before Jelena. These girlfriends gave me more and more confidence. It's sad to me that they will read this and think that that's all I am (and that that's all they were to me, rat-a-tat-tat, tit for tat), some sort of machine for reproducing tragic romances and exciting moments. I was something with them and we did something that must have mattered. I don't think the people I have been in love with have been arbitrary. This girlfriend is a story about not being in love.

They sat in a Chinese restaurant in Chinatown in London-town.

London Chinatown is too petite. I wonder what the Chinese people who work or live there think about it.

Water wondered why he was drawn back to these places. The food was never very good, and unless you ordered everything on the menu you were in and out within an hour. The only dish he liked was barbecued pork and duck on rice, but he was on a date and didn't want to disgust her by sucking fatty duck from its bones. Many nights he had retreated to eat mixed meat with plenty of hot chilli after searching the bars of Soho for pretty faces that showed signs of intelligence or interest in him.

Searching for mixed barbecue meats. Spit roasts. Duck.

He met Diana at a friend's party, of course. Drunk, he had managed a series of amusing remarks, which she had laughed at almost too much. So he leant over and kissed her. They kissed for hours at the busy party, pausing only to acknowledge the departure of Water's friends. She apologized for not fucking him that night, and after giving him her number and reminding him of her name, drove home in her red car as the sun rose. Water didn't think about Diana that day but a week later, four days really, he called to ask if she wanted to do some more kissing. Unsure of where to meet, connected on a noisy mobile line, they agreed he would come to her house in the afternoon. There they talked little, had sex at 4pm and went for pizza afterwards. Water didn't think he would ever love her but enjoyed her intelligent company and having sex with her. She seemed cool about it.

She was a vegetarian with a small appetite. He ordered spring rolls with some sweet and sour pork to follow.

He remembered the greasy battered pork balls, often gristly, with their polystyrene cup of orange-coloured sauce. The takeaway Chinese food of his childhood.

He remembered his father and him going to an all-you-can-eat Chinese in Montreal, the repulsion he had felt at the many trays filled with gaudy food tasting of nothing. Water steadied himself.

'What do you think, Diana?' he asked.

'I am thinking about something I shouldn't tell you.'

'Tell me.'

'It's embarrassing.'

'Don't tell me then, I don't care.'

'I wrote a story about the first time we met, for a short story competition.' Water couldn't see why this would be embarrassing.

'Can I read it?' Water didn't care that much if he did. He knew Diana wrote well but after the first few times they had been together he had lost interest in whether she liked him or what she thought of him.

'Let's see if it wins.' She said this with an attractive confidence that suggested it might.

So many writing women. I write about so many writing women, the girlfriends of Water. I think I must be thinking I'm Gertrude Stein. Perhaps writing and fucking are interchangeable here.

Sitting at the table with its white paper cloth, the meagre dishes assembled in front of him, the container with soy sauce and toothpicks at the ready, Diana lively opposite him, Water thought of nothing but his own bored irritation, a sense that he would rather it was all over. But he did like her, not hate her.

So he decided to make the best of it. He tucked into the fried pieces of pork in their gloopy cornflour-thickened sauce, with their irrelevant garnish of chunks of raw red and green pepper.

All the time, couples sit in Chinese restaurants discussing the food.

'It's not bad, how's yours?' he asked, looking optimistically at her plate of stir-fried vegetables in a watery sauce.

'Delicious. I'm not that hungry, though. Do you want some of mine?'

'No.'

Sadness showed on her face. Water had seen it occasionally before but had not wanted to know more.

He plunged in this time. 'You're thinking about your old boyfriend or something, or just sick of me, probably.'

'No. You're great. Really. It's nothing. I'm just being silly.'

'Tell me the truth,' said Water, thinking he sounded ironic.

'It's an awwwful story. He's a nutter. No, he was just screwed up. He could be very sweet sometimes and the next minute he'd be screaming at me.'

'Sweet and sour boyfriend.'

'You don't want to hear this?'

'I do.' He didn't.

'We went out for five years. You're the first person I have kissed since we split up. Shouldn't have told you that. He drank a lot. A bottle of wine every evening. His mother died when he was young, and his father was a bit of a bastard. He's a film critic. It was bad, one day, without any warning, he just called me up and told me he couldn't see me anymore. It was like being run over. Listen, I'm talking on and on, and you're sitting there just wanting me to shut up so you can eat your food.'

'No, no. It's interesting. Why did you stay with him if he was such a loony?'

'I don't know. I was obsessed with him, really obsessed. He said he needed me. He used to phone me in the middle of the night, crying and begging me to come over.'

'Sounds good.'

'Wasn't. I'm stopping talking about this. I'm over it. I talked about it so much to my friends that they banned me from mentioning him. You're nice.'

'I am not sure about that.'

Water woke up with Diana in her small but well-located flat. He never met her friends, her brother or her parents. The only person he and Diana had in common was the acquaintance who had introduced them at the party. Water had a sore back from sex and sleeping on a bad mattress. He wanted to go home, have breakfast by himself and sleep alone in his comfortable bed. He had no liking for Diana. He wished she would leave him alone. Water asked politely whether he could use her shower.

I am a bad-tempered asshole, can't stand being touched sometimes. The same embrace I desired so much becomes as bad as being suffocated with a pillow. Melodramatic. It's fucking context again. I've known this for about as long as I've known anything clever.

She laughed: 'You're so well-mannered. Of course you can.' She tried to kiss him playfully, but he turned away.

'I'm dirty. I'm grumpy in the mornings. I need a shower.'

The last time they met was outside St Pancras Station, the most beautiful in London. It was a hot night. They had been at an exhibition of young artists, including Water, which Diana had curated. All night he had not spoken to her; she had avoided him. Her friends looked at him; his asked him to point her out. The

woman whom Water had sex with but was not his girlfriend, who
was a writer and curator.

They finally spoke as the people filed out of the show. No, he
did not want to go to the party. They had a conversation amidst
the night crowd of King's Cross. Water looked around anxiously
at drunks and drug dealers. Diana cried uncontrollably. They went
back to her house in a taxi which she paid for. In the morning she
was OK, so he left and did not see her again.

10

In Rome I was happy. So I miss it. My friend Charles, like most or all of my friends, is insignificant. When I die I shall regret not having been more loyal, but I don't have enough energy to love my friends as well as my girlfriends and my family. This is just before I left Rome. This book seems back to front, upside down, backwards and forwards. Its own internal logic? Truth to subject? I doubt it.

Charles and Water walked through the park. They passed Water's favourite fountain. It was just a mossy lump spouting water in a green pond. Charles Time was born the same day, month, and year as Water and ran cross-country for his county. He was smaller than Water and had a quiet voice.

'Charlie, look.' Water pointed at one of the many couples entwined in the sunshine. 'They look like fucking snakes. They are in fucking jeans. Unbelievably stupid and ugly, and hot. Why don't they just get naked and finish it off?'

Charles and Water had met at Oxford. Charles had told Water's girlfriend that Water was arrogant, not the type of person he got on with. Water thought it funny, but Charles was strange and Water had only liked him after they met again in Rome. Charles smiled and said something laddish.

'Charlie, you're a boring bastard with a stupid name,' Water replied.

They walked uphill and, in the distance, saw some horses parading round a ring. Water liked Charles because he always loved Water's latest painting and also helped him make any large stretchers he needed. At a party on a roof terrace in Naples, Water had made Charles's girlfriend cry, which had made Charles swear at Water for the first time. The sky had been dark and the next day hot. Water had thought Charles might fight him on behalf of his girlfriend. He had done it before, so he told Water, and Water, always scared of violence, had avoided apologizing while managing not to further incense Charles.

In the park was the Borghese Gallery. It contained both a sculpture of a hermaphrodite and some Bernini figures in marble carved into perfect skin. Water liked a painting they had of Lucretia Borgia. He liked the view into the formal gardens behind. Charles was a sculptor and loved it all.

'It's so amazing,' he gushed.

The park was green and smelled of leaves. The chestnuts were on the ground. Peanuts, soft drinks and crazy balloons were sold at kiosks. They stopped at a bar on the high side of the gardens to drink a Campari and soda.

'Charlie, I have to leave this bourgeois place. It's boring. It's boring. Very fucking boring,' said Water.

'You can't leave. You love it here. You like the food too much to leave. And Jelena.'

'Shuddup. I'm going back to London. I need to be in a big city, with big galleries, I want to be famous in the city where I was born. I want my family to read about me in magazines, and be on TV, and marry a very rich girl.'

'Stop trying to be cynical. Haven't you got a lot happening here? Stay in Rome. What will we do without you?'

'Nothing, as usual,' replied Water.

They entered a garden full of busts of important people whose noses had been knocked off by vandals. Their friend Valeria's great-grandfather was there, and it made Charles and Water proud to have such an illustrious acquaintance. There was a big shed full of bicycles and tandems for hire and a few families were strenuously pedaling about. At dusk boys in tight trousers came here to show off their car stereos to girls who made-up older. On the other side was an aqueduct beside which middle-aged prostitutes approached men wandering in the night. There was an abandoned villa with pretty terraces, that might have been a café once, and before that should have hosted parties.

When Water left Rome that first time, he and Charles had cried together in the taxi to the station. Having danced all afternoon with their drunken friends, and exchanged presents of high fragility and low utility, they wondered whether the easy bit had come to an end. The party had been in Water's studio. They forced their boring acquaintances to play musical chairs and pass the parcel, relishing the aggression with which the games were played, and distributing extravagant prizes. When Charles had been a long distance runner he had vomited or fainted in hard races, but sometimes won as well. As the time approached to leave, Water gave a speech, telling his guests to fuck off because he hated them. He travelled to Paris in a couchette with two real nuns and three other poor people forced to travel by rail because their belongings were too bulky for a cheap flight.

They were nearly through the park, but the best part was last: the view over Rome with flocks of starlings performing an aerobatic show in the darkening sky. The collective smell of thousands of small birds filled the air. After pausing to take it in, you descended into Rome, down the Spanish Steps, and the streets were moving with people walking. On his first day in Rome Water had been shown the sights by Charles and had been so delighted by the number of attractive women that he had felt like singing. They had eaten ice cream, which was the best he had ever tasted, and Water had insisted on trying to find a nightclub that evening, but it was Monday so they were closed.

11

A fancy dinner in Rome when I was on top of the tawdry world of pretty girls and success, a few months before I left. Very vulgar to be pleased with oneself. Also slipped in is how I met Jelena.

In March the nights were warm, maybe fourteen degrees Celsius, so thirteen of them sat outside that evening. The attention was on him. Lucia had dark hair, thick eyebrows. She was a diver, strong and rich. Valeria made the best of what money had not bought her. Manuela had a perfect profile with a very straight nose, fine blonde hair and large green eyes. There were seven other girls, *women*, but those were his favourites. The two men offered no threat to his supremacy for they were either ugly or talentless. Anyway it was his night, the dinner to celebrate the opening of Water's show, tonight, this evening, into the morning, everyone would talk to him and want to fuck him. Jelena had gone off in a huff again, and they weren't even really going out, so he could do what he wanted.

You had to be drunk to enjoy all the attention, to explain for the fiftieth time why you painted a picture too big for the gallery so that it poked out into the Roman courtyard.

He had chosen the restaurant, too. These rich Italians, fussy though they were, knew nothing about really good food.

Let me present you with some of my favourite foods. Do you like me?

They began with a platter of oysters, and champagne which was too warm. The gallery owner, the daughter of more intelligent parents, anxious about the arrival of her boyfriend and insistent that she had eaten earlier, had made enough money on Water's show not to be stingy for once. So he ate most of the oysters. The women refused them, except for Lucia, and he wondered whether they were avoiding some pathetic (thinking him pathetic enough to think that way, pathetic for them caring if that were the case, pathetic that people believe in the very idea) aphrodisiac.

Lucia whispered to Valeria. Water thought perhaps they still hated him, even if they admired his enormous arrogance. More likely one of them wanted to leave.

Arrogance. The quality of other people thinking you think you are superior. What's wrong with knowing you're the best?

They had no energy for celebration, and it made Water long for his ugly English friends, who would have been drunk by now and pleasingly jealous of him. Rome's night in its tight streets was all controlled culture. The restaurant they were in had wood-panelled walls, bourgeois couples in gray, brown and black clothes, simple tables, fish on display in the front, wine on high shelves, and medium-to-high prices by Roman standards. Water liked it because no matter how many times he had been there the waiters never greeted him more than politely.

Next they ate raw slivers of swordfish, good black olives, grilled slices of aubergine, artichoke hearts and roast peppers. There was a breeze, and they drank Pinot Grigio. There was good bread to accompany the oiliness of the starters. Water was happy. Being happy was knowing when and why you were happy. Happy Water knew that he would be famous and that these pretty women desired him, and that he was eating at one of his three favourite restaurants in Rome. So he was happy. If you could paint something no one has ever seen before you would be happy. You might even make someone else happy.

They talked about his success: 'I am just happy someone likes them. Selling a few is good as well,' said Water.

'They're fantastic, amazing, super beautiful, aren't they Jack?'

'I like the big tree like an oak tree in a wet field,' replied Jack, Valeria's Anglo-Italian boyfriend. He saw Water's face: mouth full of food, eyes eyeing Valeria's strapless expanse of tanned back, but was helpless to protest, suppressed by too many good-mannered English genes.

'Water is a genius. He is so crazy, like Groucho Marx,' Massimo said, apropos of nothing.

'Massimo, listen to me, you're beautiful and I love you but please shut up,' answered Water.

The waiter saw an unshaven man in a white suit amidst ten youngish women and two self-effacing men, and was momentarily unsettled. Water shouted in English. The waiter waited to place gnocchi with clams and linguine with lobster, on the table. Water wanted a better wine, the most expensive they had. His happiness was so extreme that he worried it might become misery. He thought that if he could eat enough, and fuck Valeria or Lucia or

Manuela, he would be OK, and anyway his show was good and
the curators from London and New York had come and left with
an idea of his genius, *Flash Art* would review it, and the good
collectors had bought it. It was enough. Basta. Gnocchi with
clams, the food was very good he thought.

Rome was a good city to begin with. Its beauty provided
competition for ambitious aesthetes. The Borghese Gardens with
their trees in the sunshine, and the view of the hazy city uniform
but for its domes and Victor Emmanuel monument. Filled with
lingerie shops and good restaurants and bars with tidy sandwiches
and the best coffee. Handsome people without much sense of
purpose. Monogrammed towels, sex and love half-hearted. At its
centre a Roman temple opposite a McDonald's.

These descriptions are making me sick. Time Out *guides, Sunday
supplements, blah, blah, blah.*

Manuela was on her mobile. She was sad today. She had told
Water about her problems earlier, when he hadn't really listened,
distracted by the straightness of her nose. She would always be
unhappy, whatever infidelities her boyfriend and she did not
commit: it was this that made her beautiful. She was quite stupid
too.

Two perfect T-bones hulked on wooden boards. Only Lucia
and he had wanted a second course following the pasta. One
steak was actually enough for three. They were char-grilled on
the outside and bloody inside, served with lemon and some roast
potatoes to soak up the juices. The less robust could not look.
Water thought Lucia should have been sexier with her husky
voice and taste for rare beef, but she was not interested in Water.
Water thought fuck her (he wouldn't), he would be famous. She
would regret her contempt.

Friends and everyone else passed by, stopping to chat, refusing to stay, the women non-committal to Water's demands that they come to a disco with him. The people round the table knew everyone, anyone important or rich. So Water was happy. Born twenty-two years ago, alive for a few of them, and now with the right people and not needing them.

At Lake Braciano Jelena's slim limbs had looked good in the late autumn sunshine and he had decided to keep that picture of her in his mind for as long as he could. She swam well. She was embarrassed about the shape of her feet. She had told him not to touch her in front of her friend Mario the architect. Mario drove her round in his old car and she and Mario talked a lot about art and other serious matters. Water didn't like Mario for any obvious reasons except that he liked Jelena. Water had met Jelena at a party. She had seen him dancing after six gin and tonics. He was inviting every woman he met for lunch the next day. She had liked him. He had failed to notice her while looking for women with more exposed skin. His friend made a confused appointment with her and that's how it began.

'You fuck off,' said Jelena as they had walked to the restaurant that night of his opening. He was embarrassed by the scene in one way, but it also must have looked interesting to everyone else. She had been upset and jealous, though he heard her answer her mobile cheerily as she walked off somewhere.

No one knew whether she was his girlfriend because she had a lot of male friends. He remembered a night when she had looked at photos of all his old girlfriends with such dispassion that he thought he loved her. But Water knew it was better to try with his rich Romans tonight, a no-lose situation. Firstly it would make Jelena jealous, secondly it might be fun.

The crème brulée arrived with his Sambuca and an espresso. A combination of comfort and sophistication. Cracking open the brittle sugar, Water imagined he was haemorrhaging as he entered into the eggy custard. The Sambuca cleared his memory.

Lucia had left before dessert because she said she had work the next day; Valeria and Manuela were doing their best to be raucous. Valeria's voice was high as she enthused, 'Come on, you will do everything in the world, you know it, Water. Don't be tragic; it's very simpatico.' Water was unaware his face revealed his thoughts so clearly. Maybe his paintings did, too. Last month when he had been arguing with Jelena he had painted a picture of the two of them. With a stick he had dribbled and scratched broken images into the wet blue paint. Clouds with faces, her face covered by her hands in brown thick strokes, (she had disliked her nose as a teenager), little cartoon figures punching nothing and green grass as hair. It was a good picture that few people had admired. Valeria was right, though: he would do it all. And Jelena would probably come back.

All those days of running after her. It was a waste of time. If only she had slept with me sooner, we could have avoided all the other mess.

12

I cannot follow books with too many characters. There is one character in this book. The great big fat shit: me. But it's good to show other people. They exist, I sometimes think. Here is Charles Time. Contrast him and Maggie with me and Jelena.

Cities are either big enough to be scarily unknowable, or too small, therefore provincial and leaving one yearning for the real thing. New York is worse than London, Water thought, so he didn't live there even though he had the right to by birth. Charles Time went there with great emigration difficulty, because his girlfriend found London too inconvenient. London, with its overcrowded tubes, rain two-thirds of the year and rising crime rate, was good because it was unfinished, leaving space for ambitious people to invent it. Charles loved New York, but Water thought it too satisfied with itself and stuck still, like a sculpture.

Charles had met his girlfriend Maggie in Rome, of course. Magdalena, Maggie had an Italian-American mother and Italian father, who were rich but didn't like people pointing it out. Charles had quietly fallen in love with her. Once they were together Water had seen little of them. He didn't understand what they saw in each other. She seemed to absorb all Charles's energy. Maybe they fucked a lot, thought Water, but you never knew.

Maggie was tall (funny-looking standing next to Charles), a good tennis payer, with lots of slightly frizzy hair and round large eyes. She was vulnerable to protracted illnesses. Charles liked her plain-speaking, which she got from her mother.

This Maggie is a composite of a woman I once played tennis with, my best friend's middle name and an Australian I knew.

In New York she and Charles lived in a flat that belonged to her family. Water would have hated to be obliged to his girlfriend for a home because in an argument you couldn't say go fuck yourself without being told it was her house. Charles's strength was to not mind serving others and conversely to accept being provided for by them. He worked hard in a coffee shop, taught drawing privately to a few friends of Maggie's family and kept a studio over the river in Brooklyn. So he had nothing to be ashamed of. Maggie didn't go out to work. She was busy deciding whether or not to finish her PhD. She did the occasional translation from home for a little money.

Charles Time stood on the roof looking back towards Manhattan. A clock stood out in the night, its red digits revealing the moment. His studio, lent to him by a friend who had gone to work in Rome, was on the fourteenth floor of a building full of studios. If you climbed gingerly out his window, you stood, king over New York, on a flat bitumen roof with low edges. In his studio were sculptures ready for a show in a middling New York gallery.

Charles went there every evening he could; after he had

finished his day jobs, eaten dinner with Maggie and ascertained whether or not she wanted him to stay. Charles's sculptures were intelligent and well constructed, requiring many hours of patient work. Water told Charles he hated them because they appealed to those who admired meticulous skill and thought they had good taste (meaning they liked grey/beige).

Climbing back into his studio, Charles worried whether Maggie was all right. She had told him to go work, but she had been coughing a little, and she had kissed him goodbye weakly. Charles wanted to marry her so she would be happy and he would not lose her. Her family had grown to accept him as the boyfriend of their only child, after their initial reservations about his quietness and small stature. When Charles had met her in Rome, Maggie had had a boyfriend, to whom she was indifferent despite their relationship of three years. It had not been difficult for Charles to replace him: a lawyer living in New York exchanged for a sculptor living in Rome was a good deal romantically, if not financially. It could have been only a Roman holiday romance, but his devotion was hard to resist, and she soon depended on Charles for her happiness.

Water thought Charles had been shortchanged. Before Rome, he and Charles had been about equal careerwise. Yet in New York Charles was just a curiosity who would only exhibit in galleries which were respectable but took you nowhere. Water would never have emigrated for Maggie. Soon they would be married; children would follow to add to their happiness. Charles would need more money, and then they would be old and mediocre.

Charles never thought what Water thought. He lived in a Manhattan apartment, loved Maggie, looked forward to their wedding, was working on his solo show, was busy every day and was lucky not to be an engineer like his father. Charles worked into the night lovingly layering glue-soaked paper onto chicken-wire

armatures. From a distance they looked like knobbly sculptures but close up each bump was a small face, an immaculately painted picture of Maggie. At most, working all his spare hours, straining his eyes towards blindness, frustrating himself for six months, he could make two of these strange objects for exhibition.

When he got home from that night's labours, riding the subway in the early morning, he found Maggie feverish and weepy. Charles asked why she hadn't phoned him, and when she explained how important his work was to her, he felt like his heart would break from being too full of love for her. She was hungry so Charles heated up some soup, and served it with buttered toast cut into triangles. She couldn't eat much because her throat was sore. She fell asleep listening to Charles read aloud.

13

About Jelena. Why did I marry her?

Why did Water fall in love with Jelena? When he was in Berlin
for an exhibition, at the beginning of his success, he broke up with
her. He never understood her because she was different from him.
Berlin at that time was fresh. On the metro people smiled, they
weren't as rude as he had been told. He liked Germans: they were
more interested in ideas than the English. He was excited about
the show and his new paintings. He didn't know anyone in the
city, so he phoned Jelena, hoping to tell her his thoughts, but she
was sick and didn't care, or listen. He knew their time was up.

After that Jelena was really ill. She had bad appendicitis and a
difficult operation, with a slow recovery.

Before that, Jelena and Water had spent a week in Amalfi. It
was out of season but they stayed in the best hotel still open: a
former convent with a courtyard full of orange trees. Their room
had its own terrace, with a view of the sea, and a small table where
you could eat breakfast. There was a large bed with good linen and

the walls were white and the floor tiled. Peculiarly, the bathroom had two levels, combining a downstairs shower room and a bath upstairs. The hotel was quiet, with only a rich couple and some quasi-pilgrims resident. A plaque on the wall outside said that Wagner had stayed there once.

Or was it Goethe? I have seen this hotel since in those lame guides to the twenty best hotels in the world they have in the travel sections of newspapers.

At night, holding hands, they walked along the harbour wall. The air smelled of semen; a few stars were around. They had been happy all day.

'I hate this place, fucking Amalfi. It's dead like all of Italy.'

Jelena said nothing, she knew what was coming. Water resented all constant states. He didn't understand what to do once you were happy.

'I love you and want to die,' he declared. 'This is the first time I've ever thought about suicide.'

'You look ugly with your hair like that,' said Jelena. 'It makes you look fat.'

'You're so boring,' countered Water, awoken from his reverie.

She walked off. Water didn't care. They argued all the time, every day on average. They fought, and shouted, and hit, and he slept on the floor a lot. He would walk to the end of the wall, to see the stars reflected in the sea, afterwards he would get some pizza to take away and a cold beer, then he would find her or go to bed and lie awake, waiting.

She had cried a little and gone to buy some nice things for their dinner. They went to sleep mutely that night.

The next day was sunny. They went down to the beach and Water insisted on swimming in the cold sea. A child wearing a

Pokemon costume was running about with his father.

Water had bought Jelena a very expensive swimsuit with the last credit available on his MasterCard, but she refused to put it on, so they had another argument and she walked off again. They never got tired of being angry.

In the afternoon they met on the cliff paths above Amalfi. They sat together on a wall in the sunshine. Jelena showed him the worms crawling over the dry stone paths. She explained it was because they were by a cemetery and the worms crawled from the dead, perhaps after they were finished with them. Jelena told him she had met an old woman, a nun maybe, who asked her why she was upset and had given her some advice. Water didn't really listen, the nun had spouted the usual obvious stuff people say. He wondered whether he loved Jelena.

I hate it when people you like say boring things, thinking they're interesting.

Having spent some OK time together they argued again in the evening, woke up OK and then argued again about carrying a suitcase, or taking a taxi, or money. On the train, everybody was shouting into their mobile phones: he and Jelena were angry and silent. Water looked at Jelena as she looked out of the window. Sunshine shone on her face. He looked to see if he was able to be without her.

Romantic.

14

That last chapter seemed almost sweet. I begin to believe in what I write. Here's more Jelena. This is what happened with Jelena and Water in Rome, after the opening with the big dinner.

Water walked around the little streets, his expensive wallet full of big-denomination notes, knowing Jelena was working in the gallery nearby. Most of the important things were still to come, so he was happy. At 7pm all the shops were open for another hour. People milled around, deciding which bar to take a drink in. Jelena worked in a gallery mainly answering the telephone, but also writing press releases (which made her feel it was not a complete waste of time). They exhibited well-known British artists and the owner was the usual type of rich person who owned art and other things, like apartments and boats. It was less vulgar to run a gallery than a shop. As an enterprise it seemed more decorative than profitable. Jelena went there Wednesday to Saturday from 4pm to 8pm, which to Water didn't sound like hard work, but Jelena was always busy.

She always refused to let you phone her at the fucking gallery.

The first night she stayed in Water's bed she spilled red wine over some of his new books. But Water hadn't cared at that point; he was focused on the pursuit.

He didn't know where this was going. He was only concerned with making her love him. At each point of their relationship she had to decide how much to give in to him. Like a classical seduction, it required careful calibration of pain and pleasure, disdain and love. In those days Water imagined his future filled with beautiful and clever women, his childish vision of himself as the new Picasso. From his sisters' conversations he had learned it was not so difficult to be loved: passion, strength, a little intelligence, height, OK looks, good gift-giving, generosity, attentiveness, being interested in what they were saying. Even a few of these qualities combined would win most women eventually. It was obvious: you liked who liked you. Therefore, from the beginning he had shown off his repertoire of admirable qualities and given her lots of attention. She had been hooked, but still resisted, forcing him to greater extravagance. For him there was no risk, he believed he needed nothing; victories or defeats were only interesting chapters in his biography. Perhaps it was that inner indifference that made him attractive. He thought about his future alone, for he was too ambitious to take anyone along with him.

Water looked at the shops, thinking what he could buy Jelena to make her smile. She was always angry with him, refusing what he expected she'd like, liking things he hadn't noticed. She seemed to want to set him new standards, and Water was happy to be challenged because he believed himself invincible. For her he offered a new source of attention. In Rome they drove around a lot on her scooter, his arms around her but not pressing, he the passenger: free to see. She showed him bars where they did hot milk with amaretto, places to buy brioche very late or early, where you could get to hang out with famous Italian writers. Things he wasn't interested in but enjoyed being shown by her. He believed she had no sense of humour. She felt that he was one of many.

I was the English one.

She collected male friends, ambiguous suitors, towards whom Water felt less than his usual jealousy. She talked long and earnestly to them about herself. Unlike Water they seemed frightened of her ferocity and unable or unwilling to possess her. In the company of her men, Water could barely rouse himself to gratify her with demonstrations of jealousy. Her friends were boring. Water's mood was high and low as one day to the next she rejected him, insulted him or was pleased by him. Some flowers he sent her thrilled her, but she was dismissive of the expensive restaurants he took her to (she told him she had been to better ones). She talked of herself as though it were natural for everyone to love her. She screamed about eating too much dessert, blaming Water for ordering it. She was thin.

Not jealous. Then later jealous. You wait to show off your bad qualities. First comes the madness of wanting what you don't have.

They promised each other they would spend that summer together. But she had her tonsils removed, so excused herself from having to fulfill their agreement.

Water went back to England to busy himself with his success.

In the early autumn he flew to see her. Another airport, another arrival, back to the city he had left. They met again in the Piazza del Popolo, where they did not kiss with passion. He was angry she had not met him at the airport, and was not sure why he was

there. She was not clear what he meant to her. Rome was filled
with acquaintances he could not bear to meet again, so they went
to Napoli. She had lived there once for a few months so knew
the city and loved it. He was jealous of the time she had lived
without him. The world that he was not part of was perfected
by his imagination. The first evening they were happy as usual.
They ate and drank in the streets (which possessed all the mystery
of new places for him). Afterwards they returned drunk and full
to their modern hotel by the harbour. They had sex, and soon
Jelena was screaming at Water. He told her to go fuck herself, he
wanted to sleep, he always thought her anger manufactured. She
cried some more so he turned on the TV. She slept in the chair,
shivering all night. For her everything was first beautiful like a
movie and then terribly ugly, which confused her.

Sex and misery. Hurrah!

Every day from then on was worse, with only occasional pauses for
some tranquility on a train or walking in a park, the rest warfare
without emotional restraint. Water believed she truly disdained
him, and was uncertain how to make her like him again. He didn't
even know why he wanted to. Competitiveness or love.

Without sleep, and with many things left behind, he boarded
the plane. The airport had been OK. It was a quiet afternoon
and they hadn't made too much fuss about changing his cheap

ticket. It was calming in a way, going dazed through all the little ceremonies of air travel. He even forgot his keys in the plastic box for the X-ray machine, but a kind security man found him staring at parmesan and prosciutto in the duty-free shop, so it was not a big problem.

Airport fiction.

He hadn't known what day of the week it was till he was on the plane and looked over at somebody's newspaper. There was a silly article debunking the myth of Friday the thirteenth. Not a good day to decide to leave your girlfriend thought Water, enjoying his own wryness as he looked at the sunlit clouds, so perfect he wondered why people didn't love flying more. With Jelena he had made many mistakes, pushed when he should have pulled, but still he knew he wasn't leaving her. He had flown away because he didn't know how to be with her, and didn't want their story to end for lack of imagination.

15

More holidays from hell. Pleasure and pain. Pleasure is better, but pain will often keep us entertained. This is also what happened with Jelena.

Water wrote to her that he had left to make her love him. She wrote back to say that she did. In letters they could be calm, with paper providing a space where love's fiction could exist. When they had been together they had only been together for a few weeks at the most. They never bought the weekly groceries, or went out with each other's friends, or came home tired from work.

Actually never done much of those things. Don't like doing them. That's why I'm a painter.

Their shared life had been no more than a series of holidays. The limits of their love were defined by egotism and idealism. They could not choose to live in the same city because that would have required one of them to move for the sake of the other. They could not live everyday life together because that would have made their love ordinary and tarnished by the mundane.

You should read the letters. There are heaps of them in ugly ripped-open envelopes. Their addresses are written in felt tip, and they were sealed with masking tape, so bits of it hang off and the letters get stuck together. In fifty years they'll be in a museum case.

Where did they go? Once to Prague, where they had been lent a flat belonging to a dealer who had sold a few of Water's paintings. They expected nothing from Prague, but it was worse than that. The big dumb fairytale castle and bridge were swarming with besieging tourists. The culture Prague might once have possessed had been dismantled and carried away in the invaders' backpacks, or disseminated and dispelled by guidebooks long before Water and Jelena got there. The food suited the coarseness of Prague's destroyers: roast pig, wurst, heavy dumplings, bad goulash, scalding tasteless soup.

Jelena had been to Prague before, as a teenager on a school exchange programme. She remembered a different place, but didn't know whether she or the city had changed more. She had been the ringleader in her class, with both boys and girls afraid of her. She was always the one who would risk most, her energy and anger making her feel invulnerable. With Water she felt nostalgic for that power. He made her think about him too much, while he was shielded from her angry wilfulness by his ambition, and by having grown up in a large family. She, an only child, did not know whether she liked being so aware of somebody else's desires and moods. He loved her singularity.

They went to the museum of natural history. She looked at the cases of rocks, fish, shells, fossils and stuffed animals. Water thought it was all boring but was amused by her enthusiasm. Afterwards they continued an argument from the previous night, when Water had been so angry that his control had slipped. It was not really anger, it was an unnamed emotion which made Water indecisive, involved in a drama that he neither enjoyed nor wanted to escape. Either he liked the pain, or he should have left (but he knew he would return). Jelena screamed, cried, punched, seduced, shouted, insulted, bullied, wailed, moaned, and he did the same.

I blame her, of course.

Their stage was a borrowed flat at the top of a concrete block, amidst many other such blocks, away from Prague's hysterical centre. It was a place where a murder could occur. You reached it by a complicated route: first you went underground on the shabby metro, then on the surface you rode a bus through land covered in apartment blocks and roundabouts and motorways, where the majority of the city lived. Through the bus's steamy windows you could see a world made alien by its covering of snow. An environment so hopeless it made Water optimistic. Their apartment block could only be distinguished once you became familiar with the reduced language of the landscape. Some advertizing hoardings and a sharp turn by the bus alerted you to your stop. In that lonely flat they made war for an entire week. Every night Water slept on the floor fully clothed, prepared for the next argument. Jelena constantly declared her hatred for him, his English superiority, everything he had ever done to her. When they were walking through the Jewish cemetery he called her a Nazi. The unpleasant food they were served in restaurants was taken away half eaten (anger had replaced hunger). Instead Water ate hotdogs from kiosks until they poisoned his digestion and gave him diarrhoea. All day and through the night for seven days they fought each other, holding back only from separation. They left Prague on a train, and by Brno they knew they were safe, now they thought they could stomach anything awful between them.

The pleasure was missing.

Where else did they go together? They went to cities in northern Italy. In Modena they searched for a hotel facing the cathedral. Water imagined killing himself by jumping from the putative hotel's balcony, into the square, where the talking of the old men would be disturbed for a brief time, and then continue. Jelena said she had had the same idea. Perhaps everyone who came to Modena considered it: there were posters in the streets announcing 'Modena is Dead. Demonstration next week by the young people'. Luckily no hotels faced 'il duomo', so they checked into somewhere nearby, where the concierge scrutinized their passports and insinuated that Jelena was a prostitute. It seemed typical of the stuffy city, always fog-filled, its inhabitants dressed in black or grey. They watched TV in their room, scared of the melancholy outside, protected by each other. They talked to each other, not quarrelling for once. Jelena told Water about her childhood, and Water listened. He was not bored. They woke up neither angry nor resentful, the fog burnt off by the morning sunshine, they waited in the railway station café, drinking orange juice and enjoying the thin sandwiches.

Il dumbo.

Another city they went to was Bologna. In the busy railway station Water saw her again, a hat and winter coat failing to disguise her beauty. Water wondered how he could think she was so beautiful. She probably was, in a conventional way that might have been enough, but he sometimes saw her as beautiful as a painting. That confused him, for he believed that painting was real and that love was an illusion. They hugged in the station and she held him tight. They stayed in an enormous flat which belonged to a friend of hers. At night they went out to dinner with the friend. The streets, uniform, strong, porticoed, terracotta, gave comfort. Water thought that at last he was content with Jelena, could talk to her, be with her friends, tell her what he didn't like, be his best self. She told him afterwards she had found that time peculiar and undefined. Wherever Jelena and Water went they were out of sync. On the telephone with her in Italy (an hour ahead) sometimes they found a conversational rhythm, perhaps because she was one hour more tired than he was.

They went to Trentò. Water had a picture in an exhibition there. Contemporary art was a travelling circus stopping at the most unlikely places on the roads between the major art cities. Trento did at least attract collectors from the surrounding area who wanted to spend the profits of their northern Italian industry. The opening included a lavish buffet, followed by speeches, then dinner in the gallery where the artists who spoke English sat at one end of the table while the important local people occupied the other. Jelena was bored, but Water felt obliged to stay; there was no solution to these tedious functions. After dinner they went to a local bar where they drank cocktails and ordered some toasted sandwiches, trying to distract themselves from time passing. Jelena pretended she was engrossed in conversation with some curator, so Water flirted a little with an American artist. Jelena told him he had humiliated her. He replied that she should not be so jealous. He remembered the times she had made him jealous and hated her. The town, surrounded by mountains, was dead, shut up all day Sunday, but in the evening they found a restaurant to eat in, avoiding the other artists milling about the town, and ate quietly.

An interlude. On the phone, another jealousy outbreak. Somewhere along the the line I lost my self-restraint and once gone it's hard to find again. I wonder whether you enjoy reading this stuff. That would make you a sadist (always the possiblity I mean masochist, enjoying pain, feeling pain, cruelty or empathy, my brain finds it hard to define).

'You always lie to me,' said Water.

'Because you are a baby, I cannot tell you the truth,' replied Jelena.

'Why didn't you tell me your French friend was at that party? It wasn't even a fucking party, there were only seven of you.' The friend was a French businessman who had taken Jelena out to dinner a few times. Water was aware that he was punishing Jelena for having enjoyed herself with her friends until 4am.

'He was with his girlfriend anyway,' said Jelena.

'I just do not understand what pleasure you get from being with these rich idiots, and why you have to lie to me.'

'You cannot understand that I am happy, having fun, talking, being the centre of attention, dancing with my friends, with people who are more interesting than you. You hate me. You want me to be at home crying, miserable, waiting to kill myself over your love.' Jelena was tired, she wanted to get off the phone.

The constant beeping of her mobile disturbed the pastoral idyll. She and her friend, an expatriate French woman called Sandrine, were picnicking in one of Rome's peripheral parks, a place replete with horses and goats, which created the illusion of being in the countryside even though it was barely twenty minutes from the centre. Today Water had sent her many text messages demanding she come to him, melodramatically declaring his inability to live without her, his great passion for her. She was happy, laughing with Sandrine, discussing their lives, deciding together that she and Water were truly in love. Jelena loved Water. Sandrine photographed her next to a horse, joking that she could send it to Water to see if he could tell who was who. They laughed a lot in the sunshine. Another message from Water. Jelena texted him that she knew they were really in love. Jelena and Sandrine decided to go for an ice cream, Jelena shouted she would have two. Then they would go to the opening of the new contemporary art museum, to watch all the bourgeois Romans showing off: it would be a fun evening.

'I'm sorry I was so stupid and jealous,' Water said. It was easy apologizing. 'I love you and do trust you.'

'Why do you imagine I want to fuck every boy I meet? Because you are waiting to be free from me to find some English sheep? How can I be with you, with your disgusting jealousy? It makes me not respect you. You destroy my ideals. I cannot be with such a weak man. I don't want a boyfriend.'

'If I'm without you I'll probably never be in love again. I'll be alone forever,' said Water.

'This is what I have always known. After you there are no others to love. You have only just decided this about me.'

'I'm stupid. I told you that, but eventually I learn. I'll stop being jealous. Do what you want. I mustn't control you, just love you. We'll see each other soon.'

'I am tired now. You steal all my energy for work with arguing. Love, it's too much energy. I need to be alive.'

'You are. It's OK,' said Water.

Phone calls, letters and holidays lead to unsuitable marriages.

They were in London twice. The first time Water showed her everything he knew and Jelena noticed what Water had not seen as exceptional before. He was the host, thinking ahead, where to go, what to do. The view from the bus on a rainy day, Regent's Park: its ducks and boats, and big green space. His real life in London would have been a poor show. They looked at his favourite paintings, went to parties he hoped would be glamorous, took the train to Kempton Park to watch the races, rode in buses and taxis and tubes in order to see as much life as possible. She was happy but didn't tell Water, so he thought he had failed to entertain her. She wouldn't talk to his friends because she was ashamed of her imperfect English. She went home, leaving Water out of sorts.

The second time was hell. He picked Jelena up from Heathrow airport. Her plane was delayed three hours and she was interrogated by customs about her reasons for coming to England. Water spent the entire week complaining that he couldn't afford to pay for everything, or that he was tired and wanted to rest, couldn't she spend some time by herself. She told him his house was disgusting and dirty, that he was stingy, an idiot and a sadist. They argued each morning, spent all day apart and guilty, and were unable to be happy in the evening, resentful of the day's failure. At Heathrow going home he told her to fuck off, launched her luggage trolley into the crowds, and walked off. She had told him once again how much she didn't need him and that he should have paid her airfare for making her come to his dirty house on this miserable trip. After that she was ill in Bratislava, seriously, in a way Water had not expected. She had something like glandular fever, but worse, and he, and perhaps also her doctors, weren't sure exactly what it was. She blamed him and his dirty country for nearly killing her.

16

Breaking up was always easy for me. At most a couple of weeks of melancholy followed by hunting for women again. After I broke up with Jelena, I got bored with the ego ups and downs of trying to pick up chicks, and was ready to do something new, which I hadn't done before: that is, get married. But I'm jumping the gun. This bit is about splitting with her.

When they were together he liked the uncertainty of the future, which they did not discuss, preoccupied by their present. He always forgot what she looked like, refusing the aid of photos.

Jelena was proud of her Slovakian roots in a way Water did not care for. He sneered at her nationalism. She told him not to believe everything he read in Western newspapers. Their worst arguments were about politics because she was angry about being forced to ask permission to live in Italy, and Water could live where he liked.

She lived in Rome and he lived in London when they were going out, but the distance did not make them think of living in one city. For all the letters Water wrote to Jelena, he never considered making his friend Charles's mistake of moving somewhere to be with his girlfriend.

Jelena found the world exciting. Riding round Rome, she missed her home, but was exhilarated by the great and small elements of the city. She had worked hard to reach this position (studying at the ramshackle Roman university, earning money in a gallery with her part-time job) and was already attracting attention from editors and journalists who were impressed by her intensity. Her stories of life in Bratislava during the transition from Communism were included in an anthology of young writers from the former Eastern bloc, which had been translated into English. Drinking an amaretto and hot milk, demanding the barman make it hotter or complaining that the brioche was stale, she seemed to belong in Rome.

She was insulted by people thinking she cared what they thought, though she valued the approval of the powerful more than she would admit. She believed in Water because of his high ambition.

She had a sense of limited time that made her demand perfection and scorn people she considered weak, not hesitating to tell them directly what she thought of them. She was liked by many people because she was pretty. She drank, without often getting very drunk, smoked and told stories and decried her fate. Water sometimes called her by the affectionate name her parents used: Lenka. But he never had time to develop his own name for her.

Water often told Jelena how much he hated all the silly boring people he met. He sat brooding at her friends' parties, seeing he could gain nothing, and angry that Jelena spent her time with idiots. Jelena encouraged Water's contempt for the world, in the belief that the value of his love for her increased in proportion to it. Water felt he was Jelena's puppet, his jealousy and pride exerting so much force on him that he could never be sure of any other emotions. He did not realize that his girlfriends had to find any weapons they could to combat his self-absorption.

When it was all over, Jelena kept a reserve of Water in her. She imagined the slight smile that would have crept onto Water's face as he listened to her friends' intelligent observations. She knew that Water, or his absence, would remain with her forever: his endless judging of everything was stuck in her head. Jelena raged that Water had any hold over her, and then cried sentimentally (he would always be her man). Water hated fairy tales because fantasy and sentiment seemed like other forms of obfuscation to him.

She woke early, unable to sleep late as she was too full of nerves and energy. She ate astonishing amounts and then nothing. She had to finish off all the chocolates or eat six oranges and four bananas in a row. She did not know when to stop. She could tackle anyone fearlessly but not control her desire to repeat simple pleasures, smoking, drinking and eating. This tremendous strength combined with such crazy surges of appetite made her easy to love.

I thought this.

She lay on her bed in her small room in an apartment in the north of Rome, eating pistachio after pistachio, with a whiskey and hot milk beside her. She read Water's letters, dreaming of a perfect life: a big house in the sunshine with a nice garden and their three children playing, their dog barking, them laughing. She knew Water was in London. They were not together. So she cried a lot and was relieved, her energy released.

There. I attempted to imagine what another person feels.

17

Success. Success. Showbiz. Celebrity. Fame. Success. They're not bad. They're worth aiming for. If not, what else? This is when I came back to London and got on the road to success. Met my gallerist.

On a Thursday night at a packed opening in London, Water knew he could not happily be himself without a few beers. People didn't realize that he was nervous walking into the crowded gallery. Like surfacing after jumping into a swimming pool, you had to get your bearings quickly or you'd panic and choke. To survive you had to name faces and greet and move and talk about yourself sincerely and modestly. The alternative was silent disgust and no career.

This was where you took your chances, where you showed you were the kind of person people wanted to show. A lot of losers hung round the scene, but some of them became winners, so you couldn't be too dismissive about anyone or take the status quo for granted.

'I want to have a look at the show,' said Water, wanting to rid himself of an acquaintance, Michael, who talked only of the art world but enjoyed no success.

'I'll come with you.'

Small paintings of toys hung neatly on the walls of the project space of the gallery.

'They're meretricious, aren't they?' said Water.

'What does that mean?' asked Michael.

'It means they're crap,' replied Water.

'You're so critical. You're just jealous because you can't paint like that.'

'I'm jealous, that's right. This guy's a genius and he'll win the Turner prize in five years. And I'll be teaching foundation in a provincial art school, you're right.'

Fortunately an artist's band was playing punk so his rant didn't carry far in the heaving room.

'I like them,' replied Michael, with inarguable finality.

'This is Michael, Catherine. He knows a lot about art. I just need to get a beer. I'm really thirsty.' Water pulled a face for his friend Catherine and left. Getting away was the trick at openings.

The gallerist, Anna Martin, was talking with her boyfriend who was much younger than she was. She was not ugly, in a way: red lipstick and smart suit showing cleavage, lots of dark hair with a nice grey streak. Water had occasionally wondered whether it would be worth going out with her.

'Hi, how are you, Anna?' he asked.

'Great. How's it going, Water?' The gallerist (Water could never see her as much else) had a transatlantic accent which Water liked. Water told her how much he loved the show and that the gallery's new space was fantastic. Soon she turned her attention to someone else, but before she slipped off she told Water to bring some slides of his new paintings by the gallery, because she'd like to take a look. Water casually replied that that would be nice.

Not being himself had paid off. He drank another beer. He hated the stupidity of everyone, the ugly way that only success was success, that if you were negatively critical they thought you were depressed, not realistic. The beer was kicking in: he wondered why his thoughts were still so adolescent, while other people seemed to have settled into the world. He knew he would show in Anna's gallery now, she saw his arrogance and liked it. Showing with her would mean he was set up. After that more and more would come – Berlin, Paris, Milan, New York, cool shows, group shows, galleries, institutes, museums. Anna was rich. Her ex-husband, with whom she was still friends, was a big curator. Her gallery sold to all the major collectors, and she only added one artist every year to her team.

And how had he found favour with her? One of his tutors, who became one of his friends, was one of her artists. He – her artist, his tutor – had told her that Water's paintings were 'interesting'. As a result of that recommendation she had looked at Water's paintings in a couple of shows, noting him for the future, and that night had been reminded that it was time.

It didn't happen like this.

Success was always too simple. Only failure complicated matters, making you think what you were doing was wrong. Michael found Water again.

'Talking to Anna Martin, I see,' he said.

'Yeah, I like her,' replied Water, casual now.

'People say she's a real bitch; she sleeps with all her male artists.'

Water glanced around, he didn't want anyone associating him with Michael's comments, or Michael himself, for that matter (Michael was neither cool nor rich).

'That's just rubbish that jealous people say. Look Michael, I've got to go and get my coat before they close up. I'll see you in a bit.'

'Where you going after?' Michael called after him.

This reminds me of a Jilly Cooper book set in the art world. When I was a teenager I liked her civilized sex scenes.

18

More success. Sex cess. I have fast-forwarded you from the first time Water knew he was going to do it, to later on. Actually not much later as it doesn't take long to get ahead.

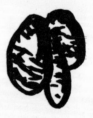

At twenty-five Water's career was good. His first solo show had opened in New York. He was nominated for major prizes in England. His profile appeared in style magazines. He knew everyone, loved no one, and painted with conviction. He sat in his studio in the morning sunshine waiting to be bored enough to paint well. Water and twenty or thirty other artists worked in the old factory by the canal that carried only swans. Some of his studio mates showed, others had day jobs (part-time or more), the lucky ones taught what they knew in art schools, many were middle-aged and had given up on fame or success, a few optimists (or masochists) still tried hard. The successful knew each other. Even they didn't earn that much. Near his brick block were other solid buildings filled with artists striving or just carrying on. A few warehouses were still productive in the economic sense: with people slaughtering poultry, roasting peanuts, or printing pamphlets. The artists acted as the vanguard of the middle classes, with the industrial space transformed into living, service and retail units as property prices rose. It was an old story. Hundreds, maybe thousands of artists were out there in London and Water was one of the few who made enough money to pay tax. His studio was the biggest on the block. NATHANIEL WATER was written in large black oil paint letters on his door and inside the TV was on low, and the radio played pop music with lyrics about love.

His sofa was covered in books, and the whole room was packed with paintings, making the 1,500-square-foot studio (about the same size as an entire London flat's floor space) seem overcrowded. Paints in big tubes, linseed oil, turpentine, white spirits, liquin for quicker drying, palette knives, flat, round, small, large brushes, plates and pots for mixing. The floor was covered in a mess of newspapers, magazines, scrappy drawings and discarded paintings. The smell was overwhelming when you first walked in, so the windows were kept open, even in winter. Water was languid. Yesterday he had done a good painting so it would be difficult to do another today without repeating himself. He sold nearly everything he painted but wouldn't compromise by letting painting become work. He watched TV, amazed by the images with their endless variation. They challenged painting's stillness.

TV is very stimulating. Painting is better. I spend more time watching TV than I do painting.

That week a painting of Water's was to be sold at auction for the first time. Water had been to the auction house to see his painting, a dangerous thing to do, for it paid not to seem overly concerned with auctions, where estimates might not be reached. His painting hung amidst others by some of the most successful artists of his time. New art already looking used. The warehouse contained installations of junk, videos playing in objects, photographs that could be shown in museums and paintings that would sooner or later be worthless because they were no good. It seemed that this place was where the fun stopped. Water saw his painting was meant to sell for four times what it had been sold for two years previously. In five years it would be worth more than a small Matisse. In thirty it might be getting dusty in a gallery's storerooms.

He had been back from New York one week. The gallery had put him up in quite a good midtown hotel. It indicated his rising status, as galleries liked to save money, even on new stars. He had shown not in the enormous space the gallery had recently moved into, but in their smaller next-door project room. It was where they tested the market for foreign imports.

His time in New York was hectic, making sure the paintings had arrived OK, trying to get them hung the way he wanted, meeting collectors, journalists, other artists, going to parties and dinners, and then it was over. Most of the paintings had sold before the show opened, and it was the kind of show insiders recommended to each other.

A primed white canvas was leaned against one wall of the studio and the sun cast a pretty pattern of shadow onto it. Water loved blank canvases before they were covered in messy paint. He began to draw figures on the rough canvas. The pencil wore down quickly. His drawings were ugly and lifeless, so he stopped. He thought about later. There was an opening at his gallery where he

would have to be upbeat. Friends and acquaintances had become indistinguishable. They knew he had some power, a few favours to hand out. He had even noticed his close friends listened more carefully to what he said. It was what was called 'respect'. Or arse-licking. The same people were always around doing the same things. Drinking, having fun, dancing, gossiping. Painting was good. That's where it all began. He reasoned: if he could do some good painting the evening would be OK. A friend knocked on his door, then pushed it open without waiting.

'Hi Water, you going to the opening tonight?' she asked.

'Not sure.'

'Tell me before you leave, so we can go together if you are. I've got my car today.'

Why were they always carving up your day? Couldn't he just be left alone?

'All right. What do you think of my new painting?' Water asked, though he didn't care about her opinion. He couldn't resist the potential for approval.

'I like the other ones better,' she answered. Water was shot down. Why couldn't this idiot see how good his new work was? (Water always thought his latest painting was the best ever.)

'What do you mean?'

'They had more energy. The new ones look like you don't care.'

'That's what I want. A careless mess which is also perfect.'

'The old ones have more of that.'

His friend left, having destroyed Water's last remaining enthusiasm. He began to paint.

Painting (verb) is thrilling.

19

Same period as the last chapter. After Jelena, before Harriet. A chance to see Water with his family taking him down a peg or two.

If you go by train, west from London down to Cornwall, all the way until the track runs out, you will end up in Penzance, close to where the land runs out at Land's End. You will have passed many dull towns and villages, gone over one spectacular bridge, caught glimpses of red cliffs and the sea but mostly just seen divided-up fields moping under grey skies. If you are lucky the train will be punctual, keeping to its generously allotted six-hour journey time.

It would have been quicker to drive but Water didn't know how. Water's mother couldn't drive either, so her living in Praa Sands, twenty minutes by car from Penzance, didn't seem practical. In Praa Sands (which was a post office and convenience store, a pub, a pitch and putt, and some houses) lived old people who wanted a view of the sea and not much else, but one of Water's sisters and her children were also there with his mother. In summer there was the occasional summer's day, but even then the sea was too cold to swim in unless you had never been anywhere hot. The rest of the seasons were uniformly wet and windy. The average temperature was slightly higher than the rest of Britain, so the vegetation had tropical delusions.

The house his mother had bought was an experiment in lower property prices, trying to live in Cornwall by the sea. When Water was younger, just before his parents had divorced, they had all driven down to look at a Cornish house with its own private beach, but they had driven back very fast in his father's Volvo, and the purchase of the house had fallen through. There were few Cornish people in Cornwall because the only business was tourism, really. The young people had left to seek work and urban pleasures. There was always a heavy resentment about, an absence of happiness or friendliness, which newcomers felt keenly and long-term residents had probably grown accustomed to.

It had been all right there for a year. Water's nephew was jolly, and a large garden flourished under his mother's care. From the upstairs window you could see nothing but sea. You could hear its waves and winds throughout the thin walled house.

Water's mother, sister and her children collected him from the train station. He was depressed from too much reading on the train, and wondered what he would do for a week in Cornwall. After only talking to rapt audiences in London, he did not know what to say to his family.

'Hello mother, hello sister, hello nephew, hello nieces,' he said.

'Hi Nat. We had a terrible time getting here. The road into Penzance is partially flooded, and Felix is teething,' his sister Polly reported.

'How's the house coming on, Mum?' asked Water.

'Terrible. The new floors are warping because it's raining all the time so they can't dry out. The roof got damaged in the gales. I am going to sell it in the summer when it will show better.' Water's mother usually started with the bad news.

They piled into the messy car and drove back to Praa Sands along unjammed, unflooded roads, choosing a route after much debate between his sister and mother over which was quickest. On the train, forgetting what he knew, he had felt like he was entering a magic kingdom at the end of the earth. After St Michael's Mount, a castle on a hill sitting in the sea, was Penzance. Seen from a distance, it looked to be a town of English prettiness. The drive home took a bypass which went through the ruined country of superstores and petrol stations, and out-of-town business parks, roads cutting through one-chip-shop-towns, or passing care homes.

Ugly. Wrecked Cornwall. I hate the place because people have wilfully destroyed it.

'I got you a nice piece of beef for dinner. It was on special,' said Water's mother.

'That's good.' Why, he wondered, was she always so interested in these price reductions and special offers at supermarkets?

'Is my bedroom OK? You didn't let the dogs in there?' asked Water.

'No, Nat. We put your stuff in the shed,' answered his sister.

As they drove up to the house he heard the dogs shouting

inside. Entering, the smell hit him: too many dogs. One of them had pissed next to the sofa. His room, so designated because he was the youngest, stank of mothballs. His mother shouted through to tell him to be careful with the window because it was broken. His dog was over-friendly. Water patted him, making him even worse.

'Enough, Arthur, get out,' Water pointed out the door to his dog.

Water got some photos of his paintings out of his bag to show his mother and sister.

They were watching television, and his mother couldn't find her glasses to see them. His sister was holding Felix, who tried to grab them, so Water took them back, defeated.

He sat down to watch television and wait for dinner.

'Have you got a girlfriend?' his mother asked, making conversation.

'No, not really.'

'Can't find anyone?' replied Water's mother.

'There are plenty of women who would be very happy to be with me. I could fuck one every night. I am too busy with all my shows,' said Water, asking himself whether her question had some truth to it. 'What about you, Mum? You found some old gent round here to give you some action?'

'You're always so charming, Nat.' His sister joined the fray.

'It's a family trait.'

Water knew he would not speak much the week he was in Cornwall, and that he would always be vulnerable to his family's ideas. He would wake late, take the dogs for a walk, eat too much lunch, read in the afternoon, maybe play a little with his nephew and nieces, demand something special for dinner, and watch TV all night. It was what he had always done at his mother's house. It depressed him now. It used to feel necessary, like a recharging of batteries, but now it seemed inevitable only because his family together knew no other way to be. At night he lay in his bed, his radio playing softly, his stuff on the shelves, his mind asking if this was everyone's future or whether his would be different.

I am not going to celebrate Christmas or my birthday again.

20

A lecture. With the usual exaggerations.

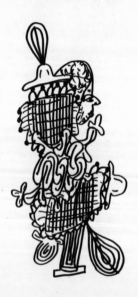

'My name is Water. Nathaniel Water. I was born in the twentieth century and will probably die quite early in the twenty-first century. I want to show you how I came to be where I am. My parents, of course, are partly responsible.'

Water stood in front of about two hundred people in one of the few galleries in London big enough to hold a decent crowd. The usual solipsism: an artist talking about himself.

'First slide please,' he said. The lights were dimmed, and the projector shuttered. An image of baby Water in a sunny swimming pool was cast on the large screen at the front. 'This is me learning to swim. It's like riding a bicycle. I was born in the USA, where my father still lives. My mother lives in Cornwall. I have four sisters and no brothers; one of me was enough, and I am the youngest anyway.' Water looked around at the audience, trying to catch an eye or a reaction, but they were hard to make out in the dark room. They stared forward or down, not wishing to be involved in Water's show.

'Why are you here?' He was bored by their indifference. No one spoke.

'I am here to talk about myself, and my paintings. You are here because you want to know something about me, or were dragged along by your friends, or just wandered in by mistake.'

Some light laughter.

He motioned for another slide to be shown. 'This is the best painting I ever did.' It was a picture of a face with too many ears. Water had promised himself to be nice.

Boring. Another slide.

'OK. Let's begin again at the beginning. I paint because I am trying to make beautiful things that people have never seen before. I want to paint as if painting had never existed, like an alien found some oil paint and a canvas and did a picture. I use traditional, old-fashioned materials because they are the most flexible things you can use, once you have learned what's possible with them. You can make any mark, any shape, any colour, any texture, any image you want with just paint and a few brushes. You don't need a computer or a camera. What I do is there for me to see immediately, and is what you see when I exhibit them. So I am an optimistic painter. I believe painting is not dead, it has just begun. When things are referred to as dead comes the point of greatest freedom.'

He did not believe his own rhetoric, but many of the people in front of him, some of them men and women who had lived twice as long as he had, were beginning to find faith in his romantic words.

Like a politician. Catchphrases. Repetition. Wanting to believe because faith makes it easier.

So he went on; the next slide showed a painting of a couple in a garden. Painted roughly, the garden, perhaps a park, appeared more beautiful than the foreground couple, who looked vulgar and out of place.

'This shows what love is. Can you see it? It's twelve feet by six, that one, oil on canvas. The best place for a painting to hang is in the home, so you can see it every day of your life without pressure. They are slow things. No one knows for how long you are meant to look at them. That's why most people find them so boring. You switch on the TV and you know what's on and when it will be over, a CD lasts sixty-five minutes or so, a book is finished when you close it, and a painting just sits there. They have no set meaning. They are not texts to be read. Sometimes they catch you, or you get a glimpse of them. Often they are the deadest objects around.'

My awful didacticism. I want others to think just what I think. Otherwise I will never stop telling them why they're wrong and I am right. When they are worn down and agree, then I will change my mind.

Water hated painting so much. He hated peddling these lies, the sort of macho talk you heard from old painters. He showed another slide of another painting.

'Do you like this one?' he asked the audience, which had expected less interaction. 'Why is one painting better than another? I don't know. Good paintings are all the same. 'Christ's Deposition' by Raphael is the same as Matisse's 'Piano Lesson', which is the same as Jackson Pollock's 'Lavender Mist'. Bad painting is not crude painting in quotation marks; it's all the painting that is not good painting, ninety-nine per cent of everything that has ever been done. There are only a few people in the world who know the difference.'

He came out with one bombastic statement after another. He was the young savant with his spellbound audience. He didn't feel like that standing there. Another slide.

'When I finished painting this I had about four hours before it was to be picked up for a show I was in. It got paint all over the gallery and you could smell it down the street. I had been arguing with my girlfriend all the time so I didn't really care about the show. I just wanted to find her a present that would make her like me.'

Back to anecdote, an easy way of eliciting sympathy and laughter.

'I got her a necklace which cost half what the painting sold for. She liked it – the necklace, not the painting – but never wore it.' Another painting. Each one nailed what he hadn't achieved, hammered home his failure. Slide after slide. He didn't want to do this again. You became a clown floundering to entertain those who could not understand.

He showed a slide of one of Watteau's 'fêtes galantes' from the Wallace collection. It showed an outdoor stage, with elegant men and women arranged in a serpentine line across the painting. The figures, despite their rococo costumes, oscillated with life, Watteau had managed to paint them to life.

Water said, 'Watteau died when he was thirty-seven, in 1721. He invented a new style of painting. It's still new. That's it. Thank you.'

My endings are never this neat. I think more about the start than the end.

21

I worry that my gloss is always so negative, and that I sound too down on myself. Don't believe it. I am great. Just that it's easy to think a thing and know its opposite at the same time. This chapter's about my sisters. Not my real ones. Extrapolations and variations. I can hear them saying the deprecating comments I write about myself. But I am sure (I hope) they don't really believe them. Ugly sisters. Pretty-ish would be more accurate.

Because Water had four sisters, it was difficult to know which one he was talking about when he said 'my sister.'

'My sister does all the big murder trials. Did you see that thing in the paper about her?'

'My sister's new novel is out next week. Do you want to come to the launch party?'

'There's an article about me in my sister's magazine.'

'I am babysitting for my sister tonight.'

His sisters seemed to his friends like one entity with many fabulous careers and beautiful children. Because the youngest was six years older than Water, they had never been anything but his sisters. Sisters, mother, father. Water understood his parents; they were part him, and their faults were his inheritance (albeit alleviated by their combination in him). Yet his sisters had his same genetic mix, so he wondered why they were subject to such irrational impulses, and willing to make so many compromises.

His sister Frances, who would courageously defend the worst murderers, could not break with her unfaithful boyfriend. It was the usual saga of betrayal and forgiveness, women loving bastards and bores, which Water would have considered too dull a story to comment on if it were not happening in his own family. The boyfriend/philanderer was not even good-looking or rich or charming. He hated Water, who treated him with rehearsed contempt, and therefore Water did not see that sister often.

His youngest sister Sarah, the novelist, was too clever. Her imagination encompassed fears and ideals that Water, if he had heard about them, would have thought a waste of time. He believed it was not worth worrying about much, events just kept happening, like it or not. In some ways it was better to be a bit stupid if you wanted to be happy and successful. When Water was with his youngest sister he was always afraid of her extreme reactions. An innocuous remark would be taken as personal criticism, or they would have to leave a restaurant or bar because someone was giving them a funny look. She could always make Water laugh though, for she saw further into the absurd and possible than anyone else he knew.

I admire my sisters. I like their collective talent and feel it reflects well on me. I am a feminist because of them.

His eldest sister Polly would also have been a painter but she had met an artist, fallen in love and had too many children. Three actually, two daughters and a son, all with fair hair and blue eyes. Maybe Polly had as much painting talent as Water had, and he privately thought that maybe she had more. Polly had not given up on the idea of being a painter, but her boyfriend was ambitious and unsuccessful. He was always working in his studio, or editing his videos, or on a residency. He earned little money, so Polly worked part-time in an art shop as well as doing most of the childcare. Water liked Polly's children; they reminded him of himself, except they seemed to draw and paint without feeling doubt, as though it were a natural part of life. Water wondered when they would grow out of it.

The other sister, Louise, was the magazine editor. She seemed worldlier, more like Water. She knew how to appear normal and friendly. Water thought she had sacrificed herself, or her intelligence, to this end. Louise was in one of those long-term relationships which no one can recall ever having been fun. Each time Water saw them the boyfriend uttered fewer syllables, and made less effort at pretending that he liked Water. His sullen arrogance stemmed from his belief that he was a great novelist who was not treated with the respect he deserved. A few of his too-wordy short stories had been published, of which Water's mild criticism was never forgiven. Believing her boyfriend's delusions, Louise was very defensive if anyone asked how his career was going. Water could not understand why Louise, pretty, successful and not old, stuck with her failed novelist.

The boyfriends don't come off well. I heard that first you're in love with your father, then you marry your brother.

Water's sisters, having known him as a child – swimming in a pool, eating prodigious numbers of sausages, stepping on a nail – never knew him as anything else. Water, who perceived so little of what made people, but saw more than he thought, was unable to tell them anything. Water's father and mother never seemed surprised by the family they had created; perhaps it was the reason they had got together in the first place.

Neat.

Christmas. Thought there were to be no more Christmases. Swore I'd stop. And here it is again. It can be taken to represent them all. An odd place to insert it, but it shows my sister, and a novel gives you the luxury of celebrating Christmas when you feel like it.

Christmas (my mother back in London having decided Cornwall was too far away): Water sits sullenly at the table; there's too much food on it, too many people round it, and a couple of dogs under it waiting for scraps. Dishes arrive, then are quickly taken away before Water can work up an appetite. Because of the numbers and temperaments the time they sit at the table has to be kept to a minimum.

Sarah tells Water not to take all the stuffing. Water replies that it is not his problem if she is not getting any. She asks where his girlfriend is. Is he ashamed to bring her home because she is too boring, or because his family is not rich enough? Water tells her, look what happened to your boyfriend. She gets serious, complaining that Water is always so unpleasant. Water says fuck off. His mother points out that Granny can hear what they are saying, and that she hates swearing, not to mention that the children copy everything the adults say and do. Water retreats into silence.

Water remembers the Christmases he has spent in Cornwall where there was no escape to his own home. In Cornwall, all of them – his sisters, their boyfriends, their children, his mother, their grandmother – were imprisoned together for nearly a week. Water would be amazed that he couldn't maintain his self-control for more than the first two hours of his stay. He hated the repetition and universality, all families, happy or whatever, performing the same play every time the cast assembled. Even death changed little, merely exaggerating the qualities of the remaining players.

A flaming Christmas pudding is brought in to ironic applause. His mother still buys silver charms which she or a sister poke into the suety ball to be discovered by the grown-up children. The real children are too young to be allowed to enjoy the risk of choking on them.

They make such an effort. If I were in charge of a party or a Christmas dinner, and someone like me responded with such rudeness, I would be furious. They carry on.

'I don't want any. I hate Christmas pudding. Is there any cheese?' Water says, not hungry, just wanting to be difficult.

'Why don't you just eat all mum's food while you're here?' replies Sarah, speaking on behalf of their mother.

'I wasn't asking you, fatso,' Water counters.

Soon dinner is over, and Water gets a lift home with Louise, her boyfriend and their six-month-old son. They leave early because the baby is tired, and Water has had enough.

See you next Christmas!

22

My mother, painting again.

Water's mother had always painted; she painted more than most painters Water knew (who spent most of their time and energy envying more successful artists). Still, she was not an artist or a painter. She had not been to art school, she did not know other artists, she had never sold a painting, she did not call herself a painter, and she did not talk like one. However, she practised painting more and more as she got older. She went to life drawing classes in Penzance (partly to see if anyone nice lived there), and she came home with drawings that looked like crude versions of Water's teenage nudes. In London she worked mostly in acrylics or watercolours because they made less mess than oil paint. Using photographs, she painted simple pictures of people and dogs. Sometimes she made postcards, which she sent to her children or lost in drawers. So she had had a long painting career without thinking of it as such.

'My mother did that. It's quite funny, isn't it?' Water said to

Anna Martin, who had noticed one of his mother's postcards in his studio. It showed some people with shopping bags and was captioned 'Happy days in Penzance'.

'It could be one of yours,' she said. 'I didn't know your mother was an artist.'

Water was wary of these easy comparisons between him and his mother. Next thing his whole family would join the art circus.

'She's not really an artist, but why don't you give her a show and then she can be one too.' Water knew this facetiousness wasn't appreciated. *She* could make jokes, but she expected Water to take art seriously. But Anna often missed his irony anyway.

'It could be interesting. A new Louise Bourgeois,' she said.

(Louise Bourgeois is a very old woman artist, who got famous in her old age with things like giant metal spiders and little drawings and prints about her childhood, sometimes sexy, surreal, etc. Exhibited at Tate Modern. First person that comes to mind when 'woman', 'artist', 'old' mentioned. In case you didn't know.)

That's how it started. Anna asked Water if his mother would do a series of paintings for a friend in New York who showed a lot of outsider artists.

Outsider artists are untrained artists who paint, draw or sculpt like trained (as in dogs) contemporary artists. Associations: Graffiti, aboriginal people, lunatics.

Water was amused, and his mother panicked: he advised her to do the same combination of elliptical sayings and crudely painted figures that had caught Anna's attention in the first place. His mother wanted to do something more polished.

'I'll do some more realistic pictures in oil,' she said.

'No, mother, stick with what they like.' Water smiled at the absurdity of advising his mother on the realities of the art world.

So Evelyn Water sent her cards to New York. She did not fly over for the opening, mostly because she hated flying, partly because it would have been too strange. She wanted to just wrap her paintings up in some tissue paper and put them in a Jiffy bag, but the New York gallery insisted on having them sandwiched in unbreakable plastic and moved by specialist art shippers. Ten small rectangles of thin card had suddenly become quite valuable, even before they had gone to market. His mother thought they were charging too much for them, but nine of them sold, with the gallerist reserving one for herself. Water's mother, who was a Water by virtue of having kept her married name, now had a career. She was nonplussed.

'When's my mother's next show?' Water asked Anna.

'I'm thinking of having her in my big drawing show later this year,' she said, checking Water's face for a reaction.

'Great. Next thing we'll be doing a mother-son talent show.'

Dealers and curators began phoning his mother, offering her shows or wanting to know who represented her. They enjoyed her ingenuous answers. Sometimes people told him an anecdote about his mother, without realizing that they were talking to her son (amazing they didn't recognize him). Others said she was a hoax dreamt up by Water: that he painted her paintings and that his mother was an actress whom he had hired.

'So what's it like being an art star at sixty?' Water asked his mother as they surveyed their first show together.

'Nat, I haven't done much, nothing really, just a couple of shows which I'm in because I am your mother,' she answered.

'Rubbish, Mum. Everyone wants you, not because we're related. They like what you do.' Water didn't know if he believed what he said. Evelyn Water's paintings were no worse than most of what got exhibited, but why her? You could probably say that about any artist, though. Water wondered if he was jealous of his own mother.

'I love painting, so it doesn't matter anyway. Maybe they'll forget about me again, but I'll still paint.'

'Don't be so pessimistic, Mum. You'll be famous longer than I am.'

'I don't want to be famous. I'd just like to have some more money so I could buy a house in the south of France, and take the Eurostar there in winter and paint. Why do I need to be famous?'

'I don't know. It might be fun.' Water had forgotten what was good about being famous. He was sort of famous, a famous young painter at least, but few people outside the art world had heard of him. He made a lot of money for an artist, though not that much for an investment banker. As a teenager he could never understand why his friends didn't want to be famous. What else could you aim for? 'Nat, you'll never be satisfied with all your success because you don't really like painting. You never did, even as a child. You just wanted to perfect it. You ripped up all your drawings because they weren't good enough,' said his mother, pronouncing upon his character in a way Water hated.

'You know everything. You didn't know you were going to become a famous painter, did you?' he said.

'I am not a famous painter,' she replied. Water decided to stop arguing and enjoy this strange moment in his family history. Drawings and small paintings by famous (for artists) artists filled the two floors of the gallery. His mother's watercolour of some birds and flowers, with its loopily written slogan: 'I know why the caged bird sings', hung next to Water's pencil drawing of some trees by a lake.

'They look quite good together, I think,' said Water.

'I think mine's better than yours,' replied his mother.

The crowd of people drinking free beer tried to pretend they weren't watching the famous son and mother.

Not sure I like this silly chapter. Could happen.

23

Moving on to Harriet at last. A relief.

Water walked around the Cézanne show angrily. As a teenager he had hated boring old Cézanne, the father of modern art. Later he had seen his brilliance, and now he was disappointed. On a London winter afternoon, Water saw nothing but old people and mothers with little kids. He hated the old people making the most of their leisure time before death. The mothers were worse, indoctrinating their children in spectatorship, the pathetic pretense that they, mothers or children, understood something about beauty. A hundred Cézannes were attached to the walls with security cameras and people guarding them, while a sparse crowd milled around. The Cézannes could do nothing to touch these people, the paintings had nothing to say. The most they could hope for was that someone might appreciate the single-mindedness of their creator, who had stared at his mountain believing he could make painting more real, better.

Water went round and round. Why did he, too, paint? His

paintings sold well, making enough money to buy a house. The market for Water was buoyant. Estimates were doubled at auction. His friends liked his work more each show he did. He could even pick new friends from anybody he wanted. He could pay an instructor to show him how to drive, and then buy a car. The Cézannes had to be looked at because a new friend, who was important in Berlin, a curator and writer, was staying with him and needed to be entertained. Water never talked seriously to her about art, or anything else. She liked Water and could help him a little. The Cézannes were as pointless as Water's paintings. At least Water knew that, which freed him.

The Cézannes showed such diligence, such a will to progress, that they made Water sick. Water never wasted his time attempting to capture some moment or vision. It was so obvious to him that painting was just painting, nothing else and nothing better. The Berlin curator, who was called Harriet (a peculiarly English name), came over to ask him whether he wanted to go upstairs with her to see the video installation. He said he would meet her up there. She had become quickly bored by these Cézannes that were considered so important in the history of art. If she, who had studied the subject and was thought to be an expert, didn't find them interesting, why expect anyone else to? He sat down, tired from dragging Harriet around London trying to impress her, and by the Cézannes which looked to him as clumsy and tedious as paintings could be. These priceless works absorbed him less than an article in a sixty-pence newspaper. *Oui oui, ennui.* A movie played, narrating Cézanne's life – the story of a boring man in a beret painting a mountain. Who gave a fuck whether he got that mountain right, or flattened the picture plane, or inspired Cubism? Water was more interested in all the lifeless people looking at the lifeless paintings. The children wailing for their tall mother, or the old folks holding hands – they were better. The Cézannes were futile. *Futile!*

Water went up to see the videos. They were expensive flat screens showing films of ordinary (actors pretending to be, or normal people acting normal) people getting on with everyday tasks in real time. Because of the startling clarity of the images produced by the technology they were immediately engaging, like views into dollhouses with real miniature humans inside. Harriet was enthusiastic. 'They're amazing, aren't they?' she exclaimed, the question rhetorical. Water knew better than to reply by criticizing the facile stupidity of the work. *Facile!* Being negative only made you look bad.

Harriet saw his face begin to sneer and flash anger, but she thought that perhaps his expression indicated some other passion. Water wondered if they would sleep together, and whether it was worth jumbling everything up. He thought there was nothing to mess up so he might as well have some pleasure. He would not love her. She could organize a good show for him in Berlin but could tell him nothing he did not know. She was intelligent and pretty and well-off and well-dressed, and Water didn't see there was much more you could want from somebody. Everybody needed somebody for a while.

At six o'clock, when people with jobs were going home, Water and Harriet came out into the dark. Water felt he could talk better, be more entertaining, if they drank, so they went to a drably renovated bar near the station and sat there, superior to their surroundings, pleased by the anonymity. They drank martinis fast. Water was surprised that Harriet wanted to. It was fun, and they began to be more personal in their conversation.

'Water, you are funny. I like the way you are always so energetic and want to go out all the time and live life. It's good to be with you. I am not trying to flatter you,' she said.

Water, flattered, knew it was necessary to reciprocate, but not too much for now.

'I'm not so great, really. You're pretty good yourself,' he said.

She talked about her boyfriend. 'It's difficult for me with Frederick living in Spain. When we see each other, there's so much pressure for it to be good.'

It was all proceeding nicely; the problem with the boyfriend etc stage had been reached already, its aim to make him a little jealous and raise the prospect of a replacement. Water thought about kissing her then.

They moved from the bar to an Indian restaurant, riding there together at the top of a double-decker bus. Their legs touched and as it turned a corner they were pressed against each other. 'This is the best Indian in London,' Water announced as they walked in. 'After, we'll go dancing, if you like,' he continued. It was important to always be fun, and maintain the constant activity, delaying the crucial moment as long as possible.

Harriet sat down and then immediately got up again to find the lavatory. Alone at the table, Water looked around at other diners, mostly young couples, or groups of friends. What other combinations of people could there be? He thought that he and Harriet made a better-looking couple than the other mismatches around him. When she returned he stood up mock gallantly, and told her he had missed her. She laughed and said, 'Frederick never stands up, even when my parents come over. He just sits there playing his music, not turning it down.'

Fuck fucking Frederick, thought Water.

Water ate carefully, wanting to impress her with his table manners, even though he acted the wild artist most of the time. They both ate and drank a lot. Then they went dancing in a bar full of people who looked younger than Water, but were probably older. It was a good moment to note, he and Harriet dancing: a jam-packed bar of conformists, the city view clearer than any painting, and the two of them free. A deal clincher.

I laugh at myself with joy in what I am.

In the black cab home they had already begun to kiss and touch. It was fun, exciting. Water remembered suddenly he had never wanted this, but it would have been strange to stop then. In his house, his house in an area where poor people still lived but where houses were getting expensive, they turned on the lights, paused, and Water politely offered Harriet a drink.

As he handed her the glass they began again and did not stop. Water was happy to fall asleep with the naked Harriet in his bed. She was elegant even in her sleep, her expensive clothes strewn across his wood floors.

24

Catch 22. Jelena again. How it ended with her and Harriet followed. Fast-pace story of Harriet romance. When someone refuses to act in their own interest, preferring to be unhappy to satisfy some skewed inner logic, they make it impossible for you to make the best of a situation. Very bitter, like the taste of burnt garlic.

People who knew nothing knew two things about him. First he was an artist, second he was getting married to a girl from somewhere in Eastern Europe. Questions they asked: 'So you can make a living from painting?' Or, more recently, just an accusation: 'Didn't I see you on TV?' Or 'Where's Jelena at the moment?' 'Are you married yet?' 'When's the wedding?' That he and Jelena had split up was none of their business. He usually just replied that the wedding was unscheduled, but that of course they would be invited.

Water put his face against the windowpane to feel the cold from the settled snow outside. The first morning it fell slowly, and everyone threw snowballs. In the night it changed the world, and the cat had walked across the roof leaving its paw prints. For two weeks it was really winter in London. Water looked into the darkness, wanting to be out there, walking through the beautiful Brueghel village that the snow had made the city. He was sad because he was alone and he knew that Jelena would never live with him. This time he called his snow period, in honour of the unusual weather. He painted only what he had to for shows. It bored him to do anything that would not be exhibited and sold. He had seen and painted so many paintings in his life, and his conclusion was that art was an entirely stupid and unnecessary activity, but he had gotten himself into it, and had to go on. He was a famous painter after all; you couldn't just stop.

It required great concentration for Water to be miserable. Surges of energy would fill him, the urge to change it all, but he forced himself to remember the futility of ambition. Listening to his words, 'I am successful enough to be depressed. No one can say I'm bitter', his friends assumed he was just missing Jelena, or speaking for effect. Between New Year and the end there had not been long. A few more grumpy phonecalls, some emails, and the fire had fizzled out for Water. It was over with Jelena, the snow had fallen, there was nothing left to argue about. He didn't enjoy her in reality or imagination. He had no more passion to love or to cry about Jelena. Initially she thought it was the same old story, the oscillation between love and hate, but the difference was that they would not be together again, so the plot had really moved on.

She phoned once more. 'So you've left me again?'

'I never left you the first time. You made it impossible for me.'

'You're trying to drive me crazy,' she said.

'I am not. You just don't get it, do you? I can't be with you anymore.'

'Goodbye,' she said.

'Farewell,' said Water, but she had hung up.

Life without Jelena.

The normal elation he got from ending a relationship was missing. Water felt no immediate desire to search for new women to pursue. He didn't want to get drunk and out of control. He wasn't even that hungry, no need to gorge himself on junk food. He watched TV and read. Some days he went for a short walk in the cold. What was Jelena doing? He didn't care. The snow turned to ice and made the pavements slippery. The pipes under the road burst, and Water's cellar filled with sewage water. It was fixed after a week, but a musty Venetian smell lingered in his house. Despite his inactivity he became no fatter. His throat became sore from the chill weather or the bacteria in his basement.

Charles and Maggie emailed, asking whether they could stay for a few days on their way to Florence for a course Charles was teaching to American kids. Water told them he would be away. He listened to the voices of his friends on his answerphone, rarely picking up except for family. If he did go out, as soon as he was bored he pretended that he was feeling unwell and left. He was sick of people and questions. He didn't want to be drawn back into the pleasurable mess of life. He deleted all Jelena's emails, which was a relief. He boxed up her letters and put them in the loft. That was the extent of his anger.

Famous Water sat in the house ordering Indian food to be delivered. It was as they said: the worst thing in life was to get what you wanted. Water had in the back of his mind that he could take a break from pushing, for he had gone far fast enough, and he knew that even if it took years for him to feel replenished, he would still restart the struggle from near the top. On his shelf were books about him and many catalogues of shows he had been in. The first book was beautiful: his name Nathaniel Water written on it. Each time he went to a bookshop he would take a quick look in the art section, and he had even found one in a second-hand shop about three months after it was published. It made him smile to see it there, shat out of the system so quickly.

The snow period lasted maybe three months. Water dated its end to when he began to have parties again. He thought how much it was possible to enjoy repetition as long as it was disguised by cycles. Rise, fall, rise. Boredom, pleasure, boredom. From the Renaissance to *Mein Kampf* and back again. He was a little disappointed that he had found no way out of it all. On a cold day, talking to a friend, he told her, 'I really don't see the point of suicide. Being alive might be bad, but being dead would be very boring.'

In order to work again he needed a new girlfriend. He had not considered Harriet as a candidate. Yet she came at the time when he was thawing out, and from a mere possibility she had turned into his fiancée, due to the grim necessity of circumstances. After the storm he needed calm. He saw Harriet as the antidote to Jelena, although from a distance she was Water's usual type, pretty, intelligent and foreign. When the snow melted, and the weather warmed, bringing pleasant Easter sunshine, Water walked hand in hand with Harriet, describing to her how beautiful her hair always looked. It seemed unbelievable that he could have ever had so many arguments with Jelena, that it had been so miserable, or that much of the time they hadn't been able to bear touching each other.

'What do you want from all this?' Water asked Harriet.

'I want you,' she replied.

'It's good to know what you want, but you can't always get it,' said Water laughing.

'You're terrible.'

'I am not. I'm with you, so how can I be terrible?'

'It amazes me,' said Harriet.

They woke up late, afternoon sun streaming through the windows, both of them tired from sex, hungry. As she got out of bed, he hugged her to him, kissed her naked back all over, and told her 'Harriet is beautiful.'

'That's me,' she said, and laughed. There were days of drifting happily: meeting in the evening, sex, waking up, eating, watching films, having a coffee. He liked Harriet. It wasn't a struggle.

25

Bored with Harriet, so I tell her I love her.

'Good morning darling,' said Harriet to Water, enjoying using the English term of endearment, then kissing him on his night-old lips.

'Morning. You want me to get up now?' replied Water.

'No. I'll make you breakfast and then we'll go out.'

Water didn't want to be made breakfast, he didn't want sex. He just wanted to lie in his bed half-dreaming, not thinking.

Harriet had been staying for more than a week, which meant Water's good humour was wearing thin, yet he remembered having assured her that he wanted her to stay for as long as she could. He was sick of doing stuff all the time.

'Let's go to the café instead,' said Water.

'I don't want to, I'll have to get dressed,' she said.

'Not for the café. Anyway, don't worry. Forget about the café, I'll go out and get something.'

Water came back with some flowers for Harriet, a newspaper for himself, good bread from the bakery, which was a bit of a walk, free range eggs and bacon that would go crispy, not just seep water and burn. He wanted Harriet to be happy.

'So what do you want to do today?' he asked her, knowing it would be better if he knew.

'I don't know. If you want to go to your studio I can meet up with one of my friends.'

'No, no. Let's do something together. I don't feel like painting.'

'I'd like to see Polly and her children,' said Harriet.

'We can do that. I'll give her a call.' Water pretended he was pleased to go over to his sister's. Harriet sat in the kitchen as he carefully fried the bacon, cracking the eggs into a separate pan so the yolks wouldn't split.

The sunlight (which he hadn't paid for, but which he liked anyway) filled his large kitchen. His girlfriend sat on one of his metal stools wearing his T-shirt. He left his eggs for a moment, to kiss her.

'You're giving me a rash with your stubble,' she said.

She always told him what he was doing wrong, but playfully, so he couldn't be angry. He kissed her again.

'We should go to the seaside. It's too nice a day,' he said. Inside with his nephew and nieces, he thought.

'What sea?' she asked.

'Maybe Brighton or Clapton, perhaps. I mean Clacton, whatever it's called. I think it's closer.' Water thought about the English seaside, and realized he didn't really need to see its sad failure today.

'What do you want from me, Water?' she cried, mock dramatically.

Water looked at her, visibly pondered the question, and replied, 'Love' – and laughed.

'You have it,' said Harriet.

They decided to go to a movie, just to be contrary. 'I can't stand intelligent American movies,' Water announced.

'We're here now; let's see a film. It is not important which one.'

'Alright, babycakes, whatever you like.'

'But promise me you won't make me guilty if you don't enjoy it.'

'I won't. I swear. Fuck! We can hold hands in the dark, and eat popcorn.'

He bought two tickets for a film he knew he would hate. They sat together in the imposed silence of the cinema. It was surprisingly full of the sort of people who thought they had good film taste but were too stingy to pay evening prices. The kind who laughed knowingly at the film's feeble ironies, and were pleased by the most hackneyed of visual devices. Water wanted to get up and shout at them. He tried to kiss Harriet instead. She gave him her hand but wanted to watch the film. What was she thinking, thought Water, how could she be interested in this crap? Water hated her. He was alone in the cinema. After a while he managed to fall asleep, waking up for the credits, his head filled with snatches of the film combined with restless dreams.

'Did you enjoy that?' he asked, even though a long time ago he had learned not to talk about films one had just seen.

'I liked the little boy; he was cute.' She knew not to tell Water she had liked it, he would only contradict her.

'What little boy?'

'You're hungry, aren't you?' It was an accusation. He was and she obviously wasn't.

He said, 'Let's go to one of those Thai places near my house.'

Her face said that she didn't want Thai. But what did Harriet want? It was such a difficult question to answer.

'All right. Why don't we go to Nando's?'

She said, 'Nando's? Is that the terrible fast-food restaurant?'

'Yes. It's not really fast food. They do chicken. I quite like it actually. Why don't we just go home? I'll make you some spaghetti or something.'

'Don't be angry, Water. We can go to McDonald's if you need to, darling.'

'If you're going to be such a snob, then I'll take you to the best trattoria in London. Which isn't saying much.'

The trattoria was a long walk away, and Water wasn't sure of the quickest way to get there, so he walked fast, heedless of the direction. Harriet hurried to keep up with him, and Water said little. His hunger made him bad-tempered. Harriet saw Water's faults as typically masculine (reminding her of her father), so she could put up with them, even *like* them.

Water went the wrong way, driven off course, he thought, by navigating under pressure from Harriet. They had to turn back and nearly start again from where they had begun. Water felt he could walk all evening without ever eating. The air was fresh, and tasted good. Why should they sit in an overpriced restaurant as though they were a middle-aged couple on a night out? He took Harriet's hand. He said, 'I love you.' He had said that funny phrase to four women in his life. Chloe, his first love, always setting an unmatchable standard through novelty. Ariane, a declamation that made sense. Jelena he didn't want to think about. Now Harriet, to whom he had run out of things to say. He was left with 'fuck off' or 'I love you', and chose the latter because there was no going back, and forwards would be more of the same. Harriet looked at him. She said it too. They walked on, spirits renewed by the magic words, fingers tightly entwined. Love was a great thing and made you hungry. Water was sure that was what Hemingway's heroes had thought. He shot himself, of course: his father had given him suicide genes.

The Italian restaurant was in a cul-de-sac. It was dark inside, claustrophobic, not like Italy. Too many candles and sad couples. The candles had burnt up the oxygen. Shelves of wine, priced for hyper-inflation, covered the walls. Water wanted to grab Harriet and flee. But already it was too late, they had a table, and had eaten a little bread hungrily.

'It's very pretentious. Strange to eat these peasant dishes in London,' she said.

Water agreed with her.

He said, 'What genuine food could you eat in London? Shepherd's pie? Fish and chips? Sausage and mash?'

She laughed. He dipped his finger in the hot candle wax then touched her bare arm. She pretended to be angry, but they had said they were in love so it was all right.

They had a bottle of red wine, which they drank quickly, as if to keep their happiness going.

The table divided them.

'What shall we do? Why don't you move to London? Come live with me,' he said.

It was flattering to be asked, Harriet thought, but her life in Berlin was comfortable. Family and friends and a good job. Water was a risky bet.

'What would I do here? I need to work.'

'You don't. You could curate more of my shows and we could go to lots of parties.'

'That would be a fulfilling life.' His gnocchi arrived with too few gnocchi and fewer clams.

'If you want there's a good bar we can go to around here. They do good martinis. You remember the first time you came to London, in that terrible bar?' It had not been long ago, but they were already nostalgic.

'I never thought you would kiss me that night,' she said.

'You didn't like me?'

'I always liked you. We were friends, remember? I wasn't sure what you thought.'

'But you weren't in love with me?'

'I don't know. You don't know until after. Were you in love with me?'

'I am now.' It was a good answer so as not to have to remember whether he had been.

'Do you want pudding?' he asked.

'We could share one.' He couldn't tell her he wanted his own, and that if she wanted one she could order it herself.

She said, 'Tiramisu?'

'That's boring. You can get the same sort of thing at Tesco's.'

'I like it.'

'We'll have it, then. You know what it means. Lift me up.'

He ordered a grappa to go with it. Harriet said she had drunk enough. Water ate most of the pudding and drank down his grappa fast because even the smell of it made him feel like vomiting. He didn't want to sit down any longer. He told Harriet they would have a coffee at home, and paid the bill.

As they left the restaurant they kissed. Water knew what to do now: he hailed a cab. The day was over, the easiness of time spent physically could begin, no more decisions, just sex and then sleep.

26

In which my father visits London. This father I write of is the mirror in which I see my defects, and admire them. This father is the mirror in which I see my future, and wish for something else.

Water's father came to London. At that time he was going out with Kay, the mother of Water's childhood best friend. (Their friendship had been unequal: Water just a toddler, his friend already playing in a baseball team. But as they were next-door neighbours it was possible.)

That his father had ended up with his early friend's mother was either a movie-ish plot twist, or the result of his father having eliminated all the other eligible women whom he was acquainted with. It seemed to Water that the world of over fifties was more lascivious than his own. Perhaps his own generation of males weren't as relentless as his father because they had absorbed some feminism. In his father's universe relationships would begin, be sweet then sour, end, and another woman would be found from amongst the available pool.

I claim I'm a feminist!

The woman – prospect, victim or hunter – would be invited over for brunch or lunch with a bunch of other friends, drink a little, not flirt noticeably, and go home full of bagels and crudités. There was no noticeable raw sexual charge or romantic banter, games or passion, nothing of what Water called beauty. Yet she would get another call, they would have dinner, see a European film, or go to a university function, and then fuck and be together, two older people who were not really sexy, or fun, or romantic. They were not stupid or without libido though, and chose each other because there was nothing else to do. You needed to be with somebody no matter where or what you were, and Water admired their still-burning drives and the efficiency with which they satisfied them.

Water's father had not brought Kay with him. Though he talked of marrying her, he probably wasn't ready to introduce his future wife to her prospective son and daughters-in-law and ex-neighbours. Water's father saw the irony in his young son – who had never had a real job in his life – owning a house worth many times as much as his own, and Water liked having his father to stay, telling him to eat whatever he wanted in the fridge, giving him fresh towels, reminding him to double-lock the doors. Water's father asked him if he had any love in his life. Water shrugged and admitted he had a girlfriend who lived in Berlin but came to stay a lot. His father commented on Water's propensity for foreign girlfriends, which was not genetic, as he kept closer to home. Water told his father about Harriet: her father was a major industrialist, she wrote reviews for a good magazine and curated shows for important institutions. His father was amused by the coldness with which Water laid out her qualities.

'Any wedding bells in the offing?' he asked. 'I can't be the only one in this family. Your sisters show no signs of marrying.'

'You're enough for us all,' said Water, not telling his father he had considered it. Why not? It would be a big party, and Harriet would be surprised if he asked her, delighted, and say yes. It would be good to finally get married after the disaster with Jelena.

Water and his father did the rounds of family and friends, and Water enjoyed taking him to openings, parties and galleries, not caring how he was thought of, amused by bringing together two separate aspects of his life.

Morandi: his father could never recall that name, so Water told him just remember a boring Moron who painted the same old stuff everyday (di). Moron ... di. Water's father wanted to be able to tell Kay what he had seen in London. Water looked at the Morandis contemptuously, some old bottles and cups in pale tasteful tones. Why waste your life never having used a bit more colour? His father dutifully tried to appreciate the quiet paintings. For Water going into a gallery was like entering a dark room, after a while his eyes adjusted and he began to see everything. The little shifts in colour, the edges, the experience and control of the sliding brush, thick and thin paint. Water then became overwhelmed by the possibility of seeing so much. The paintings became infinitely absorbing, like a madness. Now even these swings of feeling had become predictable, and their edge was lost. His father, however, was becoming enthusiastic.

'I like the way the bottles huddle together,' he said.

'In that one they look as if they are about to jump off the edge of the table, to commit suicide,' replied Water.

'I did some still-life drawings for my art class, just in pencil, but I was frustrated I couldn't get the bottle the right shape. I ended up using a ruler,' said his father.

His father insisted on getting in on the art action, always telling Water about his idea to cut rats in half and put them in formaldehyde, Damien Hirst-style, but Water thought the drawing classes had just been a ruse to meet new women.

'I don't know why you think you have to get things right, Dad. Morandi's lines are all wobbly, and no one criticizes him.'

'He's got something though,' said his father.

'You're right. He's not bad for a dull painter,' replied Water.

'Nat, you're just jealous that he's in the Tate and you're not.'

'One day I will be. Probably a few years after I have died tragically this gallery will be full of people looking at my beautiful unboring paintings, and they won't just look at bits of paint showing the highlights on bottles. My paintings have ideas and emotions.'

His father was tired. It was time to find a place for lunch.

The river near the gallery was still wide and dangerous-looking, despite its obsolescence. Water had walked beside the river many times with many friends and girlfriends. The repetition gave him a little thrill. The bridges carrying all the traffic over the water, tall red buses and trains full of commuters. Down by the banks there was development but nothing too pretty, nothing to say that business was over, now let's preserve what we've got. The river was as good as Canaletto in its detail, and more imposing, bigger to look at. Water's father wanted a pub lunch, an idea Water could not stomach: a pint with lasagne and chips or a microwaved balti. His father sentimentalized this type of food (that he would have sent back in America). Water would have liked a long lunch in a good restaurant; they compromised on an Italian café. The river, which he had not studied as he walked along it with Jelena, he would see many times in future with Harriet, and it would always offer him some solace.

27

Harriet. Good for her. I've stopped interrupting so much. Maybe I've learned to write better. Let the narrative flow.

It was always fun when Harriet came to London because she always went away again. Meeting her at Heathrow he was surprised by how pretty she was, her clear skin and shiny hair and slim figure. Immediately he could see why he was with her. She kissed him and hugged him and said how much she had missed him. They took a taxi to his house (he had arrived at the airport by tube), they had sex, and went out to a party or opening. Water felt like he had eliminated the angst from his life. Harriet's nature was determined but tranquil, so no more did Water dive from ecstasy to despondency. He had an OK happiness.

Harriet's father was doing some business in London and had invited them for dinner at his hotel in Mayfair.

The movements are strange when I write. From a lot of stuff happening all in a rush, to a story which unfolds more slowly. I don't like the linking sentences which explain the jump. They sound clumsy. In my head I go from one time, speed or place to another seamlessly.

The doorman cautiously noted Water's scruffy appearance but was reassured by Harriet's. It amused Water that these people could smell money but not recognize success.

Harriet's father greeted Water warmly. He seemed genuinely to enjoy the bohemian addition to the family, in contrast to Harriet's mother who didn't quite trust him, suspicious of Water's capriciousness.

They sat in padded chairs being served, not allowed to handle a napkin, roll, wine or water.

'I read a small article about you on the plane. Your show in Berlin is very important, no?' Mr Klinger, Harriet's father, always adopted a quizzical, slightly ironical attitude to art, claiming he was ignorant of contemporary art, even though in fact he had quite a good knowledge of art history.

'It's Harriet who made it possible; without her it never would have happened,' answered Water.

'Water's being silly. He can show nearly anywhere he wants, but he chooses to work with me,' said Harriet.

'So what paintings will you be exhibiting? More trees, or some Jackson Pollocks?' asked Mr K.

Water didn't know what to say about his paintings, that was

the problem. What were they? Water could describe everything else and any idiot could talk about their art seriously, but his new pictures were just some faces, black or brown faces most often. One reason he painted them was because there hadn't been many portraits of black people in the history of art, but if you said that it gave the wrong idea, too clear an agenda. For a start he made them up, they were not real portraits, secondly he was not operating a policy of positive discrimination to make a political point.

'Just some faces,' said Water.

'They're beautiful, Papa. Wait until you see them. They're extraordinary, and Water paints so wonderfully.' Harriet's enthusiasm pleased and embarrassed him. She was right, though, he thought.

'It sounds ... unimaginable. I hope Water will allow us to purchase one if they are not all reserved,' said Mr Klinger. It was good being with Harriet, although Water sold nearly everything he did, he never minded selling another. The rich were different; they knew more rich people.

'I would love you to have one,' replied Water, leaving it ambiguous as to whether he would make it a present.

'So I ordered for us already. I hope there is nothing you cannot eat,' Mr Klinger asked Water.

'I am totally halal.'

'Water eats everything. He's joking. He loves to eat,' said Harriet, seeing her father considering whether Water might actually be a devout Muslim.

'I thought Water was Jewish,' her father said.

'My family are mainly atheists or Church of England. The rest are Jehovah's Witnesses, Mormons, Christian Scientists, Buddhists and Sikhs. The last Jewish people in my family, in a practising sense, were my grandparents.' How boring he found answering this Jewish question, but people could never leave it alone.

'You know, our family are probably Jews. My mother always hinted at some mystery in our name. As I may have told you before, if you spell my mother's family name with a z, it is quite a common Jewish name.' Mr Klinger loved to tell Water how everyone was really Jewish, including the Ks.

Where am I from? Am I Jewish? Ask yourself what the answers to these questions might mean to you. Then mind your own business.

So they ate pâté made from the livers of pigs, served with good bread and a few cornichons.

Mr Klinger and his daughter sipped their wine and used the butter knife for the butter. Water liked eating with them. There was a calm efficiency to the way they ate, and father and daughter both had good appetites. Water gulped down his wine from his glass, already printed with his oily fingertips. The waiter filled it immediately. Water told himself to slow down or he would end up being rude to Mr K.

They discussed Mr K's trip. Mr K wanted to know if there was anything he should see in London. Mr K neatly noted down Water's suggestions, which Water had carefully considered. For all Mr K's good humour, he was very critical of inaccuracy or mistakes. It was probably why he was so successful.

'How is your wonderful mother, Water?'

'Fine. She's busy with her new house and all her dogs.' Mr K liked the idea of Water's mother. They had never met, but he imagined her as some kind of typically English eccentric.

'Why does she have so many dogs?' Mr K asked, another question without an easy answer, implying a vague criticism.

'She likes them, I suppose. The big ones are all dead, she only has five little ones now,' replied Water.

'And is she happy living in London again? Has she found a house big enough for her menagerie?' Harriet smiled and Water hated her then. He would have liked to tell this rich prick to fuck off. The answer was that of course his mother couldn't afford the big house by Hampstead Heath that Mr Klinger would have considered suitable.

'She definitely prefers London to Cornwall, even if the house she bought is a bit smaller,' said Water.

'That's good.' Mr K didn't care.

'Cornwall is so beautiful, Papa. Water took me there before his mother moved.' Harriet had been OK with his mother, though Water sensed she was a little patronizing in her enjoyment of the spectacle of his family. However, she had arrived with flowers and left chocolates, remembering that Water's mother did not drink alcohol. He and Harriet had gone on many long walks, with Cornwall showing its best face to her. Water hadn't allowed Harriet to be over-exposed to the real way his family spoke to each other, but she had seen enough to be charmed by their openness.

'Harriet liked the romantic wind-blown cliffs and cream teas. She likes Cornwall more than we do,' said Water.

More food came. Water admired Mr K's good ordering; it was what Water would have chosen.

'And your father, he is marrying again? Am I right?' It was

beginning to feel like an interrogation.

'Yes. In the summer he might marry. There are no definite plans as yet.'

'Will you be the best man?'

'The bridesmaid,' replied Water. He imagined marrying Harriet, more dinners like this one, thousands of them stretching into the future. He imagined summers and ski trips and birthdays, he imagined himself dead sooner rather than later. He looked at Harriet; there was no one better around. She was rich and not stupid and loved Water already. You needed to have someone, otherwise you were alone – which was miserable.

Water tried to take charge of the conversation by saying the opposite of what he was thinking. 'I am looking forward to staying with you during the Berlin show.'

'We won't disturb you. I know you will want to concentrate during the hanging of the show.' Water knew Mr and Mrs K would be constantly introducing him to their friends, and Mrs K would be so extremely solicitous of his needs that he would have no peace, but he did enjoy their lavish parties and the apartment (more like a whole block) where he and Harriet practically had their own wing.

They were allowed to choose their own pudding. Water had cheese. Mr K didn't drink coffee, so Water didn't have one either. Mr Klinger had scheduled a trip to the theatre that evening. Water's father would have wanted a sleep after a three-course dinner, but Mr K was still spare and driven; he had more energy than Water. Harriet was the same. Mr K apologized and hurried off to find a taxi.

Dinner with the faintly insulting prospective father-in-law. Like a job interview. Searching for the right answers to dumb questions, and I know one day I'll snap and be myself (that is, too rude). It's crazy that I call him Mr Klinger and can't talk straight to him, just because he's older than I am. He told me to call him Max, but I refused.

28

I try to be unfaithful in Rome, where I am having a show. This chapter begins with bumping into two old girlfriends in a short space of time. It happens.

It was another warm night in Rome. Harriet was in Berlin and Water was bored. He knew this show in Rome didn't really matter; he was doing it more as a favour to Valeria, who had worked on one of his first solo shows. That had only been a few years before but everything had changed since then. Success had made him important and there was no going back. As he walked towards the gallery through the mazy streets near the Tiber, he recognized a woman he had once dated.

'Hello, I'm Water. Do you remember me?' He didn't know her name now.

'Of course, Water. How are you? Do you still live in Rome?' He had slept with her a couple of times. Her English had been terrible then, and it had never been clear why she hadn't wanted to see him again. Perhaps she had had a boyfriend.

She was half-Romanian, half-Italian. After they had slept together for the first time she had chain-smoked most of the night while Water slept contentedly. Her name began with C, he was sure. Water invited her to come to his show, but she told him she was leaving Rome for the weekend and wished him good luck. She had always been outside of Rome when he had tried to phone her, and between bad mobile connections and her English, it had been too difficult to keep it going. He had waited for her once in the Piazza Navona when she had been more than an hour late, but the delicious expectancy of seeing what she looked like (he had recklessly asked for her phone number in a darkish club where she worked as a cloakroom attendant), the scrutinizing of every face looking for hers, was a memory of perfect suspended happiness. The last time he had seen her was on the metro from her apartment: she was a student like everyone else under thirty in Rome. She had blue eyes and dark hair. She had told him she would cook him a nice dinner the next time they met. He had kissed her goodbye.

Doubled the number of times we fucked. I remember when I was about ten asking my uncle whether he'd ever had a one-night stand, and he got angry, and asked me whether I knew what it meant. I didn't. It's a silly sort of expression and I can't see why it's so important, whether you fuck once, twice or thrice.

'Try and come see the show,' he said.

They politely parted, brushing their faces together, and she was gone without a name.

Her name was Carmen.

At the gallery Valeria was busy phoning journalists about his show. Rome was tedious. The people and the place never changed. Eternally boring.

Water wished he was alone somewhere in a big city working in a crap job, or writing a novel. He didn't want to be an exciting young painter any longer. Alicia, an old girlfriend whom he had gone out with for two months or so, arrived at the gallery with her boyfriend, a journalist for an Italian art magazine. Water had not spoken to Alicia for years. Her boyfriend was ugly, too big, with oversized features. Water looked at him nonchalantly. He would be writing about Water. Water, Gianni, Gianni, Water. Introductions, a brief interview and then they were gone. Alicia looked well. She had a nice mouth. He remembered her sentimentality, wanting to hold his hand when he wanted to be alone.

I meet someone I had a two-month stand with. I love these coincidences. Takes me back to being young, and I remember the thrill of the chase, and forget the dull failures, and want to go out again and pick up women.

Valeria looked at him to check his reaction. Water had made sure to control his expression, but noted her interest. The paintings he was showing were probably worse than the ones he had been doing two years previously, but were considered better because they looked more certain. Water thought they had become stale. He knew that if you changed your work too often or too much it was taken as a sign of not knowing what you were doing. Repetition was purpose.

Later Valeria and Water went to a party, and Alicia and Gianni made another brief appearance. Everywhere forever the same party with the same cast played in Rome.

Valeria leaned over to Water; she was a little drunk. 'You know, the happiest time of Jelena's life was when you were with her in Rome.' Valeria knew everyone, including Jelena. And now she was going to tell him about her.

Nothing kicks my dignity harder than being told about my personal life by a friend.

'Really,' Water replied. Everyone seemed to know their story. Jelena had cried it around Rome.

'She loved you so much.' Water thought this truth-telling vulgar; it had a hint of chastisement about it.

'It was a good time. We both had a good time. Both of us decided how it would be; it was a good time,' he said. Valeria looked offended and changed the subject. Perhaps she thought he had said, 'I had a good time'. Valeria didn't understand anything, anyway. She was jealous of Water's privacy; it was as though she expected him to open his heart to her. Those words, 'the happiest time of her life', stayed in his head, though.

Water was soon restless. He remembered when he had loved these parties, dazzled by the pretty women and foreignness of Rome. Now he had Harriet in Berlin and nothing to prove. But it was better before. He had liked looking for women, boasting, drinking, dancing and failing.

He took a big glass of vodka onto the deserted terrace. There wasn't much interest in the panoramic view of the Roman night

sky. They had seen it before. Valeria was standing there alone. Her boyfriend had left the party early. Water smiled at her, wondering if she was upset. Why not, thought Water, she looks quite pretty now. He approached, and instead of asking her what was wrong, took her hand and held it. Between them, for a moment, was a perfect romance. He let go of her hand, and began to fiddle with the silk scarf she wore round her neck, a prelude to the kiss he felt inevitable now. She smiled, teasingly asked him what he wanted. 'Nothing,' he replied, 'just looking at the beautiful moon.'

For a while they just stood there with Water playing with her scarf. Before the kiss they stood, with movements like the bobbing and weaving of paralysed boxers, but nothing happened; the kiss was never landed. Friends of Valeria came out noisily to see what was happening, spoiling the moment with their awful nosiness, killing the opportunity for something pretty. They told him Valeria was drunk and needed to be taken home; they wanted to take her away from him. He felt like a naughty child who had let everyone down but didn't understand why.

He phoned her the next day. Harriet was forgotten, and Water's relentlessness was aroused. She was feeling sick and tired from the night before, but she agreed to meet him for an aperitif at a fancy bar. Water calculated that she had wanted to kiss him, but had resisted for some unknown reason. They had a drink and were polite, and made some conversation with each other, and then she went home.

At the gallery he felt a little charge with her. It was not absolutely clear, so Water asked her out to dinner the night before the show opened. She thought he had meant her boyfriend as well, and that it was a wonderful idea for a few of them to meet up.

On the next day he just asked her straight, 'Do you want to kiss me?' It was around four o'clock in the afternoon and she was embarrassed, and said, of course, 'I can't, Water. I have a boyfriend.'

29

Me with Charles Time. A walk through London this time. He is not the good version of me. He is a mystery.

Charles and Water walked through the rubbish-strewn streets near his house. The smell of rotting vegetables was in the air. The market had not been cleared up yet. Water hadn't seen Charles for a year, but he was just the same.

Water tried to seem as confident as he had been before. Charles was always over-grateful for everything Water or anyone gave him, but maybe that meant he cared for nothing really. He was in a rush to get back to Maggie in New York, so he was only spending a week in England, a few days at Water's house.

Water had thought of recommending him to his gallery, but decided against it because Charles's work wasn't cool enough, and it would have been a waste of time and hope. Anyway, he was getting along fine, teaching part-time at a university and working hard for worthy touring shows with laboured titles.

They walked down a perfect street, preserved in its solid

Victorian elegance – unusual for London not to have everything – mixed up, more like Rome. Each house had large, shuttered windows opening into well-proportioned rooms. In a few steps they were out of the nice bit with its expensive houses and into a housing estate more rundown than most, hulking and untouched by sunlight, a reception centre for the luckiest of immigrants.

'Pretty, isn't it? You don't get this kind of beauty in Manhattan,' said Water.

'No, no. I miss it,' replied Charles.

'It's pretty shit here, the same people, openings and art every day, every week. You should come back and liven it up.'

'Maggie says she might like to come for a while. She wants to work in one of the publishing houses here.'

Water knew the weight of Maggie's desires; maybe she and Charles would really come to London.

'How's Harriet?' asked Charles.

Water could have told him about how he had pursued Valeria, how Harriet bored him but kept him somewhat content, how rich she was, how he would marry her because there was nothing else to do. But it was better to be discrete with Charles who loved to tell Maggie any juicy gossip he heard, and treated his friends' confidences as little gifts to be generously given away.

'Good. Very busy as usual. She's curating a big video show in Berlin.'

They were in the City now, where London looked like a real metropolis should, though on a Sunday its emptiness made it melancholy. Water tried to see through the hard tinted windows of the big corporations. He always hoped to glimpse one of his paintings decorating an office or lobby (demonstrating an enlightened company image and a good investment too). Probably his were stored in a warehouse somewhere, already too valuable to be on display.

'You remember when we were happy and drunk in the sunshine in Rome? Playing tennis, partying with beautiful women. Eating pizza, no worries, everything before us. Do you remember, Charles? We were young!'

'That was about three years ago. We're still young. We're in our mid-twenties. That's what you'd call young.'

'Now we have girlfriends and careers, mortgages, and tax worries. It's boring. I thought it would be better.'

'You'll like it better when you look back on it. They'll write about this time as your blue period or something. They'll say how romantic it was and wish they had been here.' Charles always knew how to flatter Water's ego. It was a skill that Water admired in him.

They faced a church now, its pillars temple-like, stony, incongruous amidst the glass and metal buildings where people worked. A roundabout separated them from the shut doors of the church. Not a single car was going round it, and the sky was high and blue. Water wondered what time people worshipped: did they get up early to go, as though church were Sunday's work?

'Harriet's OK. She likes me. I can tell her what I've been doing, and she really listens to what I'm saying. Not in a stupid way. She understands subtlety,' said Water, feeling guilty.

'I'd love to meet her,' replied Charles. Water had introduced Harriet to most of his friends. She was very presentable. He didn't want to keep her to himself.

'Next time she's in New York, I'll tell her to give you a call.'

They were walking out of the City into the West End. This was a zone where other shops began to outnumber the coffee and sandwich chains (mostly closed in the City empty of hungry employees). Water thought what a pleasure it would be to anticipate a break in the day's work, sitting at your desk deciding whether to have an avocado and bacon baguette or crayfish on rye for lunch.

'When I was younger my uncle had an office here.'

'What did he do?' asked Charles.

'Business. Publishing I think. He was a dollar millionaire for a while. He's the one who taught me about betting on horses.'

'What happened to him?'

'Our families fell out. I haven't seen him in years. I think his money went down the drain. He could never stick at one thing. They moved from Hampstead to Finsbury Park when the money ran out. Now they have a couple of lodgers to pay the bills. It's good to *have been* a millionaire, better than really being one,' said Water. Charles appreciated this kind of rhetoric. Once when Water had been with Jelena he had bumped into his uncle. They had gone for a drink in a City wine bar where everyone knew Water's uncle, who was actually not a blood relation. His uncle had looked terrible, Dickensian disheveled, but still with a little of his old vigour left. He had interrogated Jelena about Slovakia, even trying out a few phrases of Serbo-Croat which he had picked up somewhere. His uncle's charm was worn thin, and he was just running through his old routine. Yet Jelena had liked him and hadn't been offended. They had all drunk too much wine, and Water had loved her.

'When I'm dead, Charles, what will you remember about me?'

'That you were the greatest, most brilliant painter there ever was. Is that OK?'

'Maybe I'll write my own epitaph,' said Water seriously.

They hesitated now, wondering whether to go look at some bookshops or plunge into the crowds on Oxford Street. Water was sick of books, in the same way as some old people are who only read biographies or newspapers because the romance of fiction has burnt out for them. He preferred to look at the ugly shops – the little stores that came and went according to fashion and finance, the big department stores that survived longer, and thus obtained a kind of dignity. They all sold crap.

'We should take one of these stores and turn it into a museum of Renaissance painting. Imagine Starbucks, Selfridges, Top Shop and Leonardo and Michelangelo. We could make a fortune on the merchandise,' Water said, filled with the giddiness of the late afternoon.

'Hasn't someone done something similar already?' replied Charles. There was nothing new under the sun, or at least someone always told you it had all been done before.

They walked off Oxford Street.

'If we hurry we can have a quick look at the Watteaus in the Wallace Collection,' said Water, remembering he felt like seeing some good paintings. Charles didn't mind. They made it to the grand house in time to be told it was closing in ten minutes but that they could come in anyway. Water and Charles rushed up the staircase, ignoring the large and brilliantly well-mannered French paintings which covered the walls.

Water wanted to see the Watteaus. There were only a couple of tour groups left in the gallery, and a few of that breed of English women who went to galleries and museums. Paintings were everywhere unlooked at, too much from the eighteenth century, ideas out of fashion.

'Look at these, Charles,' said Water to his friend, who seemed more interested in some intricate miniatures in glass cases.

'He only lived thirty-seven years. Some copied him, no one followed him.'

'What?' said Charles.

'Watteau, you idiot,' Water replied.

'I like the way the theatre is outdoors in a garden, with the people all over the landscape.'

'That's not the point. You don't understand. He lived from 1684–1721. Thirty-seven years. Look what he did.'

(Foreground/background dogs/people nature/love.) Of course I wanted to write a biography of Watteau.

30

My father thinking. The night before his wedding. A coming together of my father, my sister Louise (the tough editor one) and Charles there to act as a buffer.

Water's father lay alone in bed watching a golf tournament. He was in his condominium by the lake; Kay was spending the night at her house in a romantic nod to the old-fashioned idea of marriage. He thought he would probably not sleep that night despite taking the precaution of drinking a couple of large glasses of wine. He never slept more than a few hours anyway, even when he wasn't getting married the next day. The golf rapidly became boring as one player went too many strokes ahead of the others. He switched the TV off, then the light, and lay in the dark, the evening's food and wine sitting uneasily in his stomach. He could hear his son and daughter downstairs. Water's quiet friend Charles was also there.

Out of five children only two had been able to make their father's wedding in America. Frances had not been able to take the time off work, Sarah was afraid of flying, like her mother, and Polly could not leave the children. Water's father had accepted their excuses. He had never worried too much about his children's affection, presuming it was unconditional, but he wondered whether they had boycotted the wedding out of some misplaced loyalty to their mother.

Water's father thought about his first wedding, in London in the sixties. Impossible to remember how he had felt, just details remained: the address of the registry office, the look of the forms to be filled in, numbers, letters and dates. It had rained, and then they had been married for thirty years, a long innings. No disgrace in trying for that long. Tomorrow they would marry in a nice restaurant out in the country, owned by a friend of Kay's, but still not coming cheap. He would have preferred a place by the lake, but Kay insisted the mountains and woods were more romantic. They made him feel a little claustrophobic, that was all.

While Charles observed them with interest, Water and his sister Louise argued over what to watch on TV. They were acting at being brother and sister, uncertain about how else they could talk to each other, and a little frightened by the wedding tomorrow which would require them to reacquaint themselves with a long-ago world. Water had asked Charles to the wedding to make sure they would, in front of him, preserve some of their veneer of social normality. But Charles thought he was watching the real thing. Tomorrow would be funny, whatever happened, thought Water. It would produce nice anecdotes. Louise was grumpy because her boyfriend had not called. She had been unable to reach him all day, and now it was too late to phone. Water had been glad that Harriet was unable to come, as she was busy with the catalogue for her latest show. He would not have been able to face her enthusiasm nor her slight pleasure when she saw confirmation of her family's superior wealth. His father's house was what her father would have thought sufficient for a young couple or worse.

Water's wedding would be different, the best, luxurious. He imagined a beach in the south of France, or a grand hotel in Berlin, or someplace tropical. He and Harriet would be perfectly dressed, beautiful and handsome, there would be the best champagne and the best food, lots of dancing, perhaps a witty speech by Water, then an elegant honeymoon. It would be rich and spectacular, Harriet's father would pay, and Water and Harriet would ensure that it was right. He wanted to marry Harriet. She was good enough.

Louise's marriage had been imminent a few years ago, but there was never a budget for it, and neither she nor her boyfriend had the will to push ahead with it. His mother would have catered and held it in their house in Cornwall, but his family had made a fuss that it was too far. Anyway, none of their relations or potential in-laws liked each other. Now Louise would never marry him. Maybe they would struggle on forever, or sometime she would despise him enough to leave him, or he would publish his great novel and leave her.

Charles missed Maggie. He wanted to phone her, but he had phoned her only that afternoon, and anyway she was going out for dinner and probably wasn't back yet. Water was different with his family. Less confident, not knowing so much how to hold himself. Charles would catch him glancing around to see if everyone was all right. Water's sister and father seemed perfectly normal and nice to Charles, so he found it hard to understand Water's anxiety. Charles remembered his own wedding as the happiest day of his life.

Upstairs Water's father finally found sleep, a nightmarish, restless sleep, which left him groggy in the morning. He was moving on in a definite way. What he had left behind was no more, and much of the time it had been his choice, so it should not have upset him, but perhaps as you got older you became more vulnerable to feelings.

31

Jelena vs Harriet. A fistfight would be close. That's the sort of shit that TV makes you think of. Celebrity death match. Jelena's madder, Harriet more efficient. Forgive me for perpetuating the German stereotype, but it's true about her. So it would depend on who was angrier. It seems likely Jelena would be.

If Jelena had written a book it would have been a fairytale. A girl from Slovakia goes to *bella* Roma, finds fame and fortune, then meets a prince disguised as an artist who falls madly in love with her. They marry and live with their three children and dog, in a castle in the woods where they paint beautiful pictures and hold splendid parties. He is the best man in the world and loves her more than life itself. In reality some of this happened, except that Water married Harriet, a rich woman from Berlin. Jelena never liked Water's uncertainty. He could never guarantee that he would not change his mind, which made it hard to imagine living happily ever after with him.

'Will you marry me?' Water asked Harriet. He had returned

from his father's wedding only two weeks before, and shared only superficial details with her. What he really thought, he liked to keep private. Now he knew that he wanted this big event: a wedding. Water had not knelt down, but he had taken Harriet's hand, looked her in the eyes, and asked. Harriet's mouth had twitched. 'You're joking,' she had wanted to say, but arrested the words, reading Water's serious face. 'Yes, I will,' she said.

'I love you,' he said, holding her tight. They kissed.

Harriet had been surprised by Water's proposal. She liked it. He had stayed with her for a week in Berlin afterwards. Every evening Harriet returned from work to find Water at home (in her new flat that her father had got her), having cooked dinner, bought flowers or found her an amusing expensive little present. After Water listened to Harriet's difficulties with the artists or the printers, they would lie together as he stroked her hair, then gently he would undress her, kissing her, telling her not to worry, holding her while she fell asleep. Then they would be in bed with him awake, thinking; her oblivious, lying, resting for tomorrow's work.

Jump.

On the telephone, a month later. She asked Water what he had been doing that day. 'Nothing, just boring shit.' He had painted, met someone about a show, had dinner with a friend. It was too tedious to recount. Harriet and Water were still living in Berlin and London, their careers too strong to alter easily.

Never lived with either of them for long, probably should have gone the conventional route, living together then marriage.

The wedding grew ever more complicated, so much so that Water had told Harriet that she and her family could decide everything, which had not impressed his own mother and sisters.

'Come to Berlin and relax,' said Harriet, hoping to lighten Water's mood.

'It's impossible. I have too much work, I can't just go to Berlin every week. I need to concentrate. Don't make me feel guilty about not seeing you,' replied Water. He didn't even want to be on the phone again with this woman he was marrying.

'Darling, you're tired, let's not argue. We'll be together soon.'

'Yes. I'm sorry to be so grumpy. I'm just sick of this miserable city, every day painting more crappy paintings.'

'What else do you want?' asked Harriet, actually curious.

'To marry you and live in the south of France with some dogs, and paint landscapes,' replied Water, laughing.

Nasty liar.

32

I am successfully unfaithful to Harriet in Venice. I don't think you should feel too sorry for her. She knew some of what she was getting herself into. I should feel guilty. Hard to imagine oneself as really a bad person who hurts another person.

Water had tried to feign indifference to whether or not he was chosen to represent Britain at the Venice Biennale. It was one of the big prizes though, so he really wanted it, and his name had been mentioned a lot in the months before the announcement. His last show had been a sell-out, more than a sell-out, much better than that, every single painting had been reserved in advance by the world's art institutions and most respected collectors, one for the Tate, two for Saatchi, one for that man in Switzerland, etc etc. The prices charged by his gallery were half what his work had been going for at auction, and private collectors considered themselves honoured to be allowed to buy a painting retail. Water looked at himself in the mirror, saw that he was not even old-looking, that his great success pleased him and made him happy.

So now they gave him this. It seemed inevitable, after it happened. Even the art writers and reviewers, so cold and bored by it all, considered him to be making paintings of 'important and astonishing beauty' and 'of things not viewed before, that can only be seen in them, which dazzle even the most cynical, uplifting the spirit'. Water thought they might be right. He saw ordinary artists watching him, excited by his mere proximity; they wondered what made him so different. In Venice he would represent great Great Britain to the world, be its ambassador, designated leader of its art. Water loved his position, even managing to present himself as quite unaffected, eager to help younger, less-established artists and rediscover middle-aged painters who had gone out of fashion. People said Water was a nice man, a loyal friend, and so in love with his beautiful girlfriend.

Water always loved to arrive in Venice. Every person had to love Venice, but even that didn't detract from it. He took the train there because he wanted to prolong his arrival. He wanted to savour the anticipation of his coronation, knowing it might be better than the reality. London, Paris, a quick taxi ride from Gare du Nord to Gare de Lyon, and on the train to Venice. Across the thin rail bridge from sorry Mestre, the most excluded of suburbs, and then stepping off the train and out of the station to ride in a *vaporetto* on the Grand Canal of this perfect city. The Waters had visited once, and there was a family memory of his father being angry about paying a fortune for a slice of pizza in St Mark's Square.

Water stayed in a beautiful room with a balcony in the grandest hotel on the Grand Canal. His friends were staying in cheaper places. Harriet was arriving on the day of the opening party, and they would be going home together on the train. Now he had a few days to be alone. The Biennale was an elegant anachronism in a global market but it was still a big draw. Prizes, speeches, crowds and trade, even if it was only art, put Venice back in business. The great Water's work was to be displayed in one of the best pavilions in the park; and a queue would form outside his show, and his catalogues would sell out. If not the Doge, he was at least one of the top dogs. And he was happy.

He fucked Helen because he was bored and drunk and she was pretty with a straight nose. His hotel room was nice with its four poster bed, marble floor and balcony where you could take breakfast looking at the sun sparkle on the water. The setting deserved some action.

Cue another crappy seduction.

Their legs touched under the table. She was in Venice making a documentary about the Biennale. He allowed himself to hold her hand. Some of the other people drinking with them were important: the commissioner of his show, the critic who had written the catalogue essay, a couple of his friends (though nearly everyone was Water's friend), and various directors, curators and friendly acquaintances who came and went in the night. Helen's dress was expensive and low-cut.

'Shall we go?' she wrote on a napkin. Water was hungry, and unsure what he was going to do. It seemed a good idea to order another martini and some little sandwiches. He didn't think the others cared who he fucked. They were all at it when they could get it.

'Go for what?' he replied on the receipt. The sun had set and the mosquitoes buzzed round the stagnant canal. Water had never been unfaithful to Harriet.

The conversation between the others was about English football and the lavishness of parties they had been to, the rotting palaces and amazing buffets.

'For fun. It's boring here!'

He washed the sandwiches down with the martini.

'Will we have sex?' he wrote. She was perfect and found him funny. She was young, and her hair was nice, and he could smell its cleanness. He remembered the time Ariane and he had written each other notes at a party. Nothing had happened.

'No guarantees. Do you have any champagne there?'

'Of course. A case, and gold carpets, and a chandelier.' The whole table was watching them, more or less. We're playing consequences, Water told them.

'So why are we sitting here?'

'I have a fiancée.'

'Me too, and a husband. I am married with three children.' She was a happy person.

He rose and took her hand, announced that they were going fishing, and they walked off without looking back.

On the way to his hotel some of the alcohol wore off and Water ran out of funny things to say, though it didn't matter,

it wasn't necessary because Helen liked him more than he had guessed. Water thought about whether he would see her again, but forced himself to enjoy the present, Helen's almost-beauty, his anticipation of being in his magnificent bed with her, the unknown of touching her, and he managed to be jolly again. In the dark of the hotel room they were clammy against each other. He remembered that he wanted to be a great artist like Picasso. There were good moments when he forgot what he was doing. She was energetic. He didn't notice falling asleep. A lot of noise from outside woke them dawn-early. Water had a slight headache. She had to leave for a meeting, so no breakfast. He kissed her goodbye, the door closed, and he was in his expensive hotel room, representing Great Britain at the Biennale, a pretty woman just gone from his bed. They had been naked together. That seemed strange already.

Why? What does it matter? I was bored. Why shouldn't people have sex? Why did I want to marry Harriet, then? I thought I could do it, sometimes, when I was feeling optimistic. And Jelena. It seemed like it must be important because it was so full of emotion. I always wanted good things, just they turned out a mess. It wasn't deliberate.

33

So many chapters, too many chapters, the numbers are ridiculous. I'm on way back from Venice, facing the music of my own thoughts.

Venice was good, he thought, as he talked to Harriet. He had bought her an antique glass necklace and matching earrings. He hadn't even noticed that they were intricately composed of flowers and birds; he had just felt an urgency to buy her a present and rushed into a shop where they had been the only decent things. She wasn't wearing them but they were nice anyway.

They waited for their train to Paris in the cafeteria of the railway station. Water drank some white wine with his reheated chicken escalope and potatoes.

'Not bad. I quite like this sort of thing,' he said, sipping the wine.

'Amazing you can eat that now, after that great lunch we had.' Harriet had only a coffee in front of her. It was just before six in the evening.

'Try it, darling. It's very good with the wine!' he said, pushing a forkful towards her face.

She flinched.

'I'm really not hungry.' But she was not angry. 'Are you pleased with yourself?'

'I am the cat who got the cream. I am the king of the jungle. I am the lion,' he said, raising his arms in the air. 'I find it strange now without the attention, not being in a crowd. Being without admiration, just with you to watch me eat.'

'As you know I love watching you eat schnitzel.'

'The party was good, wasn't it? For a moment I was with everyone, important to them. And I was happy when I saw my show with the gallery empty in the morning. It was good going up there by myself in a taxi rushing along the canal. And the queues outside my pavilion. And the hotel was nice with the balcony, and that perfect pasta with squid we had.'

'Your show was the best. I loved it.' He was not embarrassed by her praise.

'And now back to real life in boring old London. What shall we do? Let's go stay at the Ritz in Madrid, though I'm bored with fancy hotels. I could buy a bigger house, maybe I'll open a gallery, or play roulette every day and lose all the money I make, but Bacon and Freud already did that. We could go to the south of France and drink champagne. I am happy. There is nothing to do. It's good,' he said.

'Maybe you could shrink your big head a bit.'

'No, I don't want to become modest. Shall we have some children? That'll keep me busy.'

'What will we call them?'

'I think a boy should be named after me, and a girl could be called Wanda, Wanda Water.' He was about half-serious. Harriet laughed.

'I can imagine a dynasty of Waters,' she said.

He was tired. That's why they were at the station an hour and a half early. He found peace in stations and confidence through eating.

'I should teach you to play cards, then we could play poker all night,' he said. He was tired of hearing himself saying these things.

'I am not a gambler,' she replied.

'What are you then?'

'What?'

'What are you?' he said, stressing each word.

'I am your fiancée,' she said. An ugly word, Water thought. They were engaged to be married. People in novels broke engagements only with terrible consequences.

'I am your fiancé,' he said, amusing himself by mispronouncing it. 'I want to get some fresh air before we get on the train.'

'I'll wait here with the bags,' she said.

'We can leave them in the left-luggage.'

'I am tired, Water.'

'We're going to be on a train for thirteen hours, we might as well enjoy some more Venice now. Come on, come with me.'

'I really am tired. I will stay. You go.'

So he did. He had meant to be nice to Harriet. But he had to do what he wanted. He would be on that train with her for thirteen hours. As he exited the station the warm air hit him and he was glad of Venice's beauty in the fading light. There was nowhere to go, though. He had been everywhere, and was sick of the hard little streets, and there wasn't enough time to take a ride on a *vaporetto*. Even if there was, it could take him nowhere new. He was sorry about his rudeness and restlessness. Harriet was good, and he missed her. He would buy her a little present, a straw gondolier hat, or some novelty sweets. He remembered there was an English bookshop not far from the station. Maybe he wouldn't have dinner on the train, to be nice to Harriet, and because he was feeling full.

In the bookshop he couldn't bring himself to buy any Hemingway or Fitzgerald, or any of the books intelligent young Americans and Germans read in Europe. It was over-handled, grubby culture, all worn out. He was tempted by Stendhal's book on love, for Harriet, but she never read what he gave her. He went through the titles over and over again as though a new book full of new ideas would appear, but there was nothing he didn't know, and besides he was only interested in things he knew already. He settled on a stale English newspaper full of out-of-date sports results and old news. The street was wall-to-wall with tourist shops, last-minute places, millions of glass trinkets, packets of nuts, extra large T-shirts, hats, light-up gondolas, a madding crowd of junk.

His Venice Biennale ended in that street. A star had crashed and its fragments were left there in blown glass and tiny lights. For Harriet, he brought water and some bars of inexpensive chocolate in gold wrappers. They were tired on the train, and slept. He had compromised by having only a plate of salami and half a bottle of red in the dining car.

I would prefer to have loved her. It would have been more fun. I am happy and nice when I am in love. Shut up.

34

Confusing, this double engagement. Basically, thus far, I was engaged to Jelena, then split with her, then engaged to Harriet. Harriet vs Jelena 2.

It looked like he'd made a real mess of his life. Once you'd been engaged once, it was hard to take the second one quite as seriously. It was feeling responsible for their happiness that made him hate a person. He always said that. It made one guilty, and it was easier to break with the cause of the guilt. Just a few days of tears, and then no more drip, drip of everyday pain. Jelena had never liked him enough. No one could, or no one wanted to. It would be unbearable to be loved that much. The natural/perverse/human response was to hate what loved you.

Like to be liked, hate to be loved.

He organized a party for his first engagement. On Thursday he told his friends that he was having a barbecue the following evening.

He couldn't bear the false and lacklustre congratulations of his friends singly; it was better to get as many of them over with at once. Most of them hadn't been able to come at such short notice, which was good (you won both ways). Jelena said she didn't care whether they had a party, but Water knew she was pleased.

It rained, so Water ended up grilling trout, salmon and T-bone steaks on the gas stove. Jelena refused to take her hat off because she was embarrassed by her new haircut. She was popular with his friends, most of whom had never met her before, and most of his sisters were there too, with various children and boyfriends. Those who came were those who wanted to come, thought Water, and that made it good. His mother and sisters gave them a set of expensive pillowcases, a French duvet cover with a scottie dog on it, towels, and a bolster. Things for their married life together, though not for now, while they lived in different countries. People asked when the wedding would be. In December, only a few months away, he answered. And where would they live after they got married? They weren't sure, he said. Water hadn't even considered this.

When Jelena and Water were finished with each other, they didn't need to say 'I am not going to marry you' or 'it's all over.'

The fact was that they could be together contentedly for at most a week, and after that not at all, or only by arguing first thing in the morning then spending the entire day apart, then quarrelling in the evening, not having sex, and beginning with an argument again the next morning. Less obtuse friends got the message after a time. Mother and father had to be told but it was a short announcement which could be slipped in nearly in passing, and the bed linen was stained with Jelena's hair dye and could not be returned and of course was not expected to be.

He told Harriet about his first engagement. With one girlfriend he was completely honest about his past, while with the next he might act as though he had been reborn sinless or at least as an amnesiac. It didn't have much to do with the person. It was a reaction to his own feelings about what had just happened, either shame for being too revelatory or self-contempt for his ridiculous old-fashioned discretion.

He admired Harriet's calm interest in his past. It was as if she thought it all made him ready to marry her, like the ever more dramatic break-ups had burnt him out enough to settle down. He told her that even his mother had said that she was worried by his inconstancy. They didn't have an engagement party, though this time Water bought a ring that cost enough to satisfy any New York heiress. Jelena had never worn her ring for more than a day. It had survived being thrown from the twelfth-floor window of an apartment block. Harriet never took her white-gold and diamond ring off, and it made Water happy to see it securely on her finger. The first engagement had always been too unclear, as though each stage – from ring to parents to party – was an attempt to make certain in public what was unsure in private. With Harriet he was reassured by the unlikeliness of a second broken engagement in such a short space of time. Anyway Harriet handled it all well and without ambiguity, seemingly much more knowledgeable about the subject than he was, despite his experience.

He didn't feel that guilty that he had fucked someone else. Sex in Venice didn't make that much difference. He had always been perfectly faithful before, with only some grey areas at the beginnings and ends of relationships. Now he didn't say that anymore: 'I have always been faithful'. He had been unfaithful. A silly word, 'faithful', inappropriate for the atheist Water. Breaking her faith made nothing really change. Like drinking or not drinking, taking drugs or not, swearing or not, it was another useless item of morality. In some way it made him feel better and freer, and it confirmed to him that he wanted to be with Harriet; even guilt hadn't split them up. The TV woman he had fucked was a nice memory.

One girlfriend of Water's had given all his gifts away to Oxfam. The handbag, the underwear, the dress. Water liked that idea. He never thought much about what was past, but occasionally he would come across a book or an old letter from a girlfriend and he would feel an unfamiliar physical sentiment of loss. He liked those moments too.

He was in no way a hedonist; pleasure was not his ultimate aim, yet he enjoyed nearly all his feelings because they were his. He imagined Jelena looking at the back of the gold Rolex inscribed 'from Nathaniel to Jelena', and wondered whether she had destroyed it (though how many people throw away gold watches?). He imagined all the romantic presents he had ever given lying in wait for him in a terrible room in hell. In another room would be all the friends he couldn't stand anymore, and in another every one of the relatives he no longer saw, busy celebrating Christmas forever. It wouldn't be that bad though, and he would get used to it.

Harriet never registered his ranting. Water told her she should read about sex because he did in order to learn more, and you could never be too good at it. He told her he wished he could feel total suicidal despair because then he would have nothing to lose and could go fight in a war. He told her to learn to cook better because they would save money on restaurants and you always liked people who could make good food. Sometimes she laughed. Water didn't remember her making him laugh. It was years since he had laughed at anything besides artfully constructed American sitcoms. Water remembered laughing in the night with his girlfriend at college, and she telling him not to be so noisy because her friend was next door. Sometimes in bed you could laugh; touching was funny. Harriet was not frightened of him, or she didn't show it. She could tell him she would love him forever. She often surprised him with her strong sentiments. It was like having a very sophisticated child in love with him. Water was shocked every time he recognized she was alive and he liked her. When he was happy, he fell in love with himself so didn't need her much, and when he was unhappy he was too busy fixing himself to be too concerned with her. He was petty and critical as well, but Harriet's efficient and busy life shielded her. She was rich enough not to depend on him.

Trying to explain Harriet. What will she be like when she is old? I expect clever, and fit for her age, and with more humour.

Water liked shopping with Harriet for her clothes. She tried on sleek leather boots while he watched admiringly and gave his opinion of them. He enjoyed the shop assistants' envy of Harriet's fine, slim figure. Water and Harriet were young, beautiful and successful. It was their golden age. At Liberty's on Regent Street they took their shoes off to enter the wedding department, a white place with white carpets for couples with clean virgin feet, or at least socks. Water reckoned with pleasure that the wedding would cost about as much as a small house up North. In Tiffany's he had more and more costly rings brought out for him to examine, and was annoyed that they cost more than his paintings. They kept having to put back the date of the wedding because of Harriet and Water's frenetic careers. It had to be at the right time in the right season. It had to be perfect. After all you only got married once, said Water.

35

Painting. Love, art and me. Art love me. Me love art.

Water hated painting. In his studio he faced some fabric he had primed for painting. He had painted so many paintings, which collectors owned or stored in warehouses, hoping for his death or good news from the auction sales. More decoration for rich people, squeezed from his talent and ambition. It was pointless, and even if he painted a very good painting there was no one worthy of looking at it. Painting a painting. The words themselves were also ridiculous. Water tried to paint what he had seen, some pigeons flying in a leaden sky with an airplane further away in the distance. Painting what you saw, painting what you had seen, painting what you had never seen, all painting was painting what you would never see.

The light was good, and it was quiet at that time of the morning. Painting was like a chore that would never end. He knew how they would turn out, or at least the limits of how surprising the results could be. Maybe call Harriet. She would be preparing for work. But what could he tell her? He was miserable? Not great news to share over breakfast. Jelena would be awake in Rome. She loved getting up early, going to her local bar for a coffee, then buying fruit at the market. She had a thrilling energy in the morning, which Water remembered often turning into a brutal, unrelenting anger. He could call her to tell her he loved her, that they should marry and be together forever, yet how silly that was when he was engaged to Harriet, and did not want to go back to Jelena's passion.

If Ingres were alive, what would he be doing? Probably not moping around not painting. His perfect surfaces would have kept him busy all day with his tiny brush. It only took Water an hour to complete a painting. Matisse and Picasso had freed the painter from hard labour, though some still chose it. But you could have as much spare time as you wanted now. He thought of his friends: they were either failures or bores. He hated them more than he hated painting. He couldn't talk to any of them. Water laughed at his self-pity. Nothing was missing this early in the morning that a little painting couldn't cure.

Painting. Therapy for disillusion.

He felt secure in his ennui. He felt an exaggerated sense of his role in the art world. It seemed as though he could see clearly what was boring, what needed changing, and it fell to him to do it. What wasn't easy to know was what he would do.

36

The Cat in the Hat. Charles Time visits.

It had been hot for a few days running in London. Unusual to get any real heat even in summer, so rain was due. You could feel the pressure, the rain breezing in, the warm air keeping it away, but not for long. Water sat in his flat. The cat who normally visited had smelled the rain coming and stayed at home. Water had all the windows and the back door open so he could get as much of the outside in as possible. Actually he was in a house, not a flat, and there were two cats that visited, both black, and hard to tell apart. Water put them in his paintings sometimes, though they would not have recognized themselves.

Charles was meant to arrive in the next hour. Water felt guilty about not meeting him at the airport, telling him to take a taxi, that he would pay for it. Harriet was away again, so Water would have to entertain Charles by himself – something he had become unused to. Talking to his friends with Harriet was easy. She was interested in them in a natural way, and liked new people. His friends were impressed by her elegance and casual charm and liked her in return.

Charles knocked on his door about midnight. Water was drowsy. He had been in bed too much recently – twelve or more hours from night to day – enjoying broken dreaming and waiting for Harriet to return. Nothing much else to wake up for.

'Charles! You're alive!' He dragged Charles's suitcase in and slammed the door behind them, generating energy for himself through his faked exuberance.

'You look great, big man!' said Charles.

Charles was tired too. Water could see he wanted to sleep, though he forced himself to sip a glass of vodka Water had given him. Charles had a meeting the next morning with a curator, and was flying to Rome in the evening for some other important business. Water had forgotten exactly what. Charles was always judging scholarships, or doing fellowships, or receiving some kind of grant. Charles would see him for only a few hours because he was so busy.

He offered to order some takeaway for him because there was nothing to eat in the fridge, but Charles had eaten on the plane.

'How's Maggie?' Water asked.

'Good. She's doing really well with her new job. I think she's finally found what she wants to do.' Water thought this was the first time he had ever heard Charles speak with the slightest hint of criticism about Maggie's short-lived vocations. It pleased him to see that even their perfect marriage was developing cracks.

'So you must tell me about marriage. You're my best man, after all.' Water plunged in: old best friends with nothing to say, trying to remember what they used to talk about, curious to know what they had liked about each other. The old context – their happiness in Rome, Rome itself – was missing. Water thought he had no friends; they didn't exist.

'I'm sure you'll develop your own way of doing it. Patience and trust, and lots of sex (with your wife!) are what make a good marriage,' said Charles.

'You're not speaking from experience, I presume.'

'No, of course not. My parents told me.' Charles's parents had been married about a hundred years and had five sons. Water could picture them still fucking energetically.

'I think the main things you need are lots of money, a couple of houses, a flat in Paris or Rome, a dog to walk and separate bathrooms,' said Water, who had or could afford most of this and considered himself one of the most bored intelligent people he knew.

'Why are you getting married?' Charles asked – a question many people had asked Water, and which at first had offended him.

'Because I want to. You should know. I choose to. Sometimes you just must do something because it is the only thing you want. I believe in it, somehow. You get married and then you're with someone forever.'

'It doesn't have to be quite that long. Maggie's parents are separating.'

'I am sorry,' said Water, struggling to think of the appropriate reaction. 'It's probably a stupid question, but why are they splitting up?' he asked.

'Sometimes people change and then they can't be with each other anymore, no matter how hard they try. And cry. It has been quite difficult for everyone.' Charles made the mood sombre.

'I'm sorry. How's Maggie taking it?'

'All right. She's much stronger than you might have thought. I'm a bit exhausted by it all, though. I've been talking with her father too much. He's very depressed, says he has nothing left, his business is doing worse than his marriage, and they'll have to sell their New York and Rome apartments sooner or later. Maggie and I'll have to find somewhere else to live.'

Water hesitated to ask any more questions, not wanting to hear any more details. Charles continued.

'Maggie's mother has a friend that her father doesn't know about. I'm not looking forward to him finding out. It'll probably drive him over the edge. Her mother's boyfriend is one of the top bankers, rich as fuck. Maggie detests him.' Charles seemed to relish the soap-operatic dissolution of Maggie's family, perhaps seeing it as a punishment for the way they had once looked down on him. Water remembered an enthusiastic, idealistic, though admittedly ambitious, Charles. He had known him in Rome.

'The poo will hit the fan when that comes out. Maggie will be OK though; she's tough like her mother. Actually, I'd like to phone her to tell her I've arrived safe and sound. I'll give you the money for the call.'

'Don't be silly. It doesn't cost much to call America anyway,' said Water, relieved that Charles was himself again and that he was leaving soon.

37

The sad story of all the dead pets we have had. Names are of course changed and qualities merged.

Monkey died two years after Arthur. Monkey had joined the family through a combination of good and bad luck. Water, at fifteen, had won £490 for predicting, on a slip of paper, the scores of three football matches. If his fourth prediction had been correct he would have bought something more expensive. The scores were not even his own, they came from a tipster in the *Racing Post*.

Monkey came with a gold chain round his neck, and was discovered in a litter of pugs that Water had found for sale in a free ads paper. Their master, Heinz, was a large German man who bred dogs for profit. His mother and sister, who had come to help him choose a pug, supported his choice of the strange creature, a hairless gray dog from China who looked like he was made of elephant skin and who had a shock of white hair on its head, and feet tufted like a pony. He had danced out of his cage into their affections, upstaging the somnolent pugs. Monkey had vomited all the way back in the taxi, and Water quickly realized he didn't want this tiny dog who would never chase sticks or go on long walks. He threatened to get rid of Monkey, but his sister paid him not to, and his mother looked after the funny dog for the rest of its life. Monkey died one horny summer, a short time after he had impregnated his own daughter.

Arthur's death came first. He was an ugly mongrel who had been born with a bent tail because of a failed abortion. His mother Rose, another of their dogs, was a bad-tempered bull terrier who predeceased her son by a year. Arthur howled and barked his loudest when he was waiting, leashed up, to go out for a walk. Rose had bitten a child once. Arthur's father was the street's dog, a setter called Rusty who had raped Rose in the woods. Water heard one pretty day in Rome that Arthur had died of old age (he was thirteen). The weather had been unusually warm that June in England, and people and dogs always died when it got hot. Arthur was a stupid furry dog with a large brown spot on his white back. One by one dogs went, a few people got cancer or rare illnesses, an occasional acquaintance died violently or by their own hand. The tragedies, small and big, added up to nothing out of the ordinary. It didn't really matter if a dog died. Water, when he was eleven, had painted two pictures of Arthur. They had surprised him with his ability to paint realistically. One sat on his bookshelf in London, and people often mistook it for his new work. The other, a picture of Arthur lying on his back, was in a portfolio case lost in a garage. It would not be looked at again, until someone threw it out, preserved it as a memento of Water's life or tried to sell it.

Before Arthur died, Water's mother told him, he lost the use of his back legs, and dragged himself to the door each time the other dogs went for a walk. He became incontinent, and his piss had ruined the low sofa in the sitting room, which he had to pull himself up onto like a seal. They didn't put him down or make him move from the sofa that he liked. One morning he was dead, his mother said, stiff and quite heavy. They buried him in the garden in Cornwall, and Water's niece and nephews knew where he had gone. It was the first dog that had died on them.

One Christmas Water asked for a white fluffy kitten, and received a Persian that went on to have three daughters. They found the Persian in the street, dead, hit by a car, near pristine but without life. She bled from her pale nose only. Her grey fluffy daughter, whom they had kept, lived a long time and then died. When Water was eleven he wanted a dog, so his mother got him a West Highland Terrier, who was cute and seemed to have more potential to be trained than their other dogs. He painted a picture called 'fucking dogs' which is what you said to yourself most of the time about them, because they were always badly behaved. It couldn't have just been bad luck and must have been a result of his family's character. Not long after they got her, the Westie got one of those incurable immune system diseases and died over a couple of weeks. It was a pity, she would have been a nice dog. There had been dogs who travelled with them on ships, who had stayed in kennels, who had been bought in pet shops, who were the offspring of other dogs of theirs, who came free, who cost a lot of money, who had been in Europe, who had lived in America even before he was born. There were thousands of photos of dogs; Water wished no more would be taken. There were many cats as well, but they were less interesting. Water could never be excited by meeting yet another dog, and his father never had a dog after he and his mother split up.

Fucking dogs. So many dogs, so many dead dogs. Not a good augur.

38

Now Harriet and I are happily married!

Downhill, Harriet was driving Water's car, as he was still learning to drive but had bought a car anyway to motivate himself. He liked watching her hands on the wheel and her foot moving from the accelerator to the brake. His wife Harriet – it seemed scarcely credible that they had got married two weeks ago. The wedding had been in London because the Berlin plan had collapsed due to the imminent separation of Harriet's parents, which would come into effect when their apartment was sold. Following the problems of Maggie's parents, it didn't bode well for marriage in general. Like many long-married couples, Harriet's parents had clearly hated each other for a long time, staying together until they decided they didn't have to bother anymore. Water had tried to be sensitive to Harriet's feelings about the break-up, though she didn't seem too heartbroken; she was busy with her new job in London and her wedding. The ceremony was not storybook: Harriet didn't wear white and Water wore a good suit without a tie, and in order to avoid too much contact between their split-up parents, they had a quick service in a smart registry office in town followed by a party at Water's house.

It wasn't so bad after all. I don't seem destined for the big wedding organized by the bride's parents. I am no good at people giving me stuff. I am too critical and ungrateful.

'What was the best thing at our wedding?' Water asked Harriet.

'Your mother's wedding cake was amazing.' Harriet looked at Water with her serious gaze.

'What do we do now we're married? Be happy together, have children, get old, and die, I suppose it's not too bad.'

'First we have to buy some food,' Harriet replied.

The sun shining through the windscreen of the car made Water feel sleepy. He didn't notice all the busy people and the ugly streets. Harriet was a good driver, and Water idly wondered what he would buy at the supermarket. It was Saturday, so it would be packed. Yet he could dream as they wandered through the grumpy throng of trolleys. Harriet was also good at shopping, remembering what was needed, and letting him ponder the meat by himself. Now she was working in London it was even better than it had been, because she was out all day and they no longer had to do touristy things like when she had been visiting. In the evening she was tired, and content to eat dinner and watch TV, or sleep or fuck. Once she had left the house in the morning he could sleep as late as he liked, and by the time she was home, he was bored with painting and eager for company.

Their honeymoon had only been three days in Madrid. Harriet couldn't take a longer holiday from her new job. It was quite a prestigious position for someone under thirty, and she and Water made a glamorous London couple, the kind other people envied. Water had been nearly everywhere in Europe, and there were few beautiful cities unpolluted by his memories of previous relationships. Madrid was Catherine. He remembered the catastrophe of that holiday with her, which had followed the brilliance of his first college visit. They hardly spoke except to contradict or correct each other in the most pedantic manner. These disasters seemed to be a recurring theme of his life, but perhaps only because they were easier to recall than pleasant times. Catherine had beautiful pale skin with veins that were visible in watery blue near her nipples. She was a vegetarian and allergic to cigarette smoke, in a way which made him want to blow cigar smoke in her eyes and eat pigs' faces in front of her. Towards the end they had got drunk on gin and tonics in a Toledo train station, and fucked angrily when they got back to Madrid, one of the few fucks that stood out from the rest as an actual event.

He and Harriet stayed at the Ritz in Madrid, right next to the Prado, fulfilling one of Water's minor daydreams about being a rich American in the 1920s. As time went on, you kept going to the same cities. The only thing that changed was that you stayed in more expensive hotels with different people, and you took more taxis and spent more money. Three days was short enough for it all to be basically perfect.

Water remembers his honeymoon by reminiscing about an old girlfriend.

After the supermarket, they went for a walk on Hampstead Heath, a place Harriet loved.

'Someone will probably break into the car and steal our groceries,' said Water.

Harriet told him not to worry. He restrained himself from mentioning that the fish might go bad, for the sunny day was not even warm. Water was just unenthusiastic about trekking round the Heath. He would have preferred to go home and find out the football results on TV. But new couples had to compromise, he thought to himself, and was pleased with his virtue. He took the initiative and took her hand in his as they climbed a path busy with other young couples and families. Water pointed out the benches with their plaques dedicated to dead friends and relatives. He made his usual speech about how he hated them because they reminded him of how boring these dead people must have been, and why should you want to think about that when you were going on a nice walk, that reading them was worse than stepping in dog shit. Harriet reminded him that he had said all this to her before, and Water was embarrassed into silence. At the top of the hill he gave her a kiss on the lips, for luck, he said. She did not wriggle out of his embrace; she didn't care that people might watch them kissing. Harriet and Water were on top of the world, with a view back over London, all the way to the triangle-topped Canary Wharf Tower, its beacon flashing in the fading light. He held her tight, kissing her with his eyes closed, noting down this moment to be recalled and feeling that pure happiness of kissing someone you'd kissed a lot, and feeling pleasure or love (without worry that it might not be love).

In the evening Water cooked a couple of non-farmed salmon

steaks. He enjoyed feeding Harriet. She was always grateful and surprised, as though each time she hadn't expected him to make her dinner. They sat at the table in the kitchen.

'Do you want some?' he asked her, opening a bottle of good white wine.

'I have a busy day tomorrow. Maybe I shouldn't.'

'Go on. One glass won't hurt you. It's good for you,' he said, filling her glass. 'What's happening tomorrow?'

'I am meeting the director, you know, and we're going through budgets and the programme for the next months.'

Water wasn't really listening, and Harriet wasn't that interested in explaining. 'I thought you were the director,' he said.

'No. I am the curator. Perhaps I told you I was the director of exhibitions. He is the director of the institute.'

'What's he like?'

'He is not even thirty yet. He has a big reputation.'

'Wow, a real prodigy,' said Water, getting up to put some music on. Harriet had put a stereo in the kitchen, and Water, with his minimal interest in music, was content to listen to the CDs she left next to it.

'What car does he drive?'

'Water, stop being silly.'

'I'm trying to be a normal husband.'

'You are an extra-ordinary husband.'

'I'm subnormal. You just love me for my genius. You're a terrible woman.'

'Water!'

Over the next week Water visited artists to select work for a show in New York. A gallery there had asked him to be a guest curator identifying the 'new themes and talents in London'. It was a bit tacky, but it gave him to chance to do a favour to some of his friends. He had long since moved out of his old studio, tired of getting there, and of the cold days in winter. Instead, in his new house (which was actually the converted end section of a Victorian factory) he used the entire ground floor for painting. It had been specially designed with a separate entrance, large floor-to-ceiling doors for getting work in and out and a wall of windows not facing the street. It had been a while since he had seen ordinary studios. For this show, which would be of no benefit to his own career, he travelled to the margins of London each day, places without taxis, tube stops or delicatessens, getting off at a deserted rail station, walking in the pouring rain along the broken pavement past piles of dumped rubbish, mattresses and burnt-out cars, to find unloved buildings containing artists. There they were, working away, in too-small rooms crowded with their efforts. He didn't even understand or like their art, it bored him with its futility.

Futile poor failed artists!

George worked on four-metre steel sheets on which he painted words in ghostly glazes of oil paint. Piles of them were stacked against the walls of his studio. His paints were neatly arranged on a small table, and there were no windows. It was a kind of tomb.

'These are fantastic,' said Water.

'I'm happy with them,' replied George.

'But they might be a little too large and heavy to transport to New York. I think they might want smaller things. Probably stuff they can sell. You know what it's like.'

'I'd like to show the large pieces, but see what you think of these,' said George, showing him some pieces of iron that looked exactly like the other paintings, only smaller.

'Those are brilliant. They'll love them in New York.' Water wondered whether George ever questioned why he spent his spare days, the time left over from the job he did for money, carefully painting words on rusty metal.

'How long will they be away for?' asked George.

'You mean in New York? With shipping, probably three months. Do you need them for another show?'

'No. I have nothing coming up. I like to have them around to refer to.'

'Of course. Well, we could take something else,' said Water.

He came in late enough for Harriet to be at home before him.

'I hate fucking trains and fucking artists,' were his first words to her.

'You had a good day then.'

'Great! How about you?'

'It was good.'

'They're so fucking selfish, these idiotic artists. I'm doing the losers a favour putting them in a show in New York, and all they do is ask me stupid annoying questions. And then I had to wait sixty-seven minutes for a train and there are no cabs round there. It's unbelievable.' Water began to laugh at his own moaning.

'Well, I am doing very well with the director, and he likes my ideas for next year, for using other spaces in London for more ambitious shows.'

'Sounds perfect. You should be in charge of this stupid thing in New York.'

'Water. At least you'll have the chance to see Charles in New York.'

'He's an asshole too. He wants to take up half the gallery with his installation. They're so greedy and conceited. Artists. They have no idea anyone else exists.'

'They are the same as all other people.'

'How wise you are, darling. Tell me more about your work. I'll stop moaning about myself.'

The next morning he felt hungover from the studio visits and waiting in the cold. He cancelled all the friends he was meant to see, told them he had flu, and spent the day doing nothing. In the early evening he began making dinner for Harriet. The simple Italian food he made needed elaborate preparation, the sauce alone (for the papardelle) requiring chicken livers, veal and pork, which he minced himself. He replayed the previous evening, thinking how bombastic he was in conversation, how he'd had sex and couldn't remember falling asleep. Why had Harriet chosen him? Of all people. She was pretty and normal, and could have had most men. Perhaps it was because he was an artist. There was no room for anyone else with him. She might have been happier with a good-natured ordinary successful person. She was stuck with him now. Why him? Her life would revolve around him, and he didn't envy her.

Dinner was very successful, though Harriet asked why they hadn't invited some friends round when he had made such a lot of food.

39

Life with Harriet continues. And painting.

Water hated other artists, all gallerists, all curators, all collectors and most of the other people who looked at his paintings. That was his secret. To please them, he had made his art into a novelty act of genius. He had painted an entire show of twelve twelve-by-nine-feet paintings, in front of a live audience, in six hours, and they were good paintings. He had shown them, the viewers, glowing paintings in near darkness and forced them to file past them one at a time, like mourners by a monarch lying in state. In one museum in Holland he had used every room but put each painting on the ceiling, so as to strain their necks.

I have done shows like these.

He had shown paintings outdoors, upside down, back to front. He had painted badly and beautifully, realistically and indecipherably, made enormous twenty-metre paintings and tiny ones, used every colour and sometimes only one. In short he had done everything he could to surprise the people he hated. Everything he could think of to make them believe they had seen something new, which was impossible because their expectations were infinite. And he despised them because they knew nothing about art. They only recognized skill or labour, nothing more, nothing that made a difference between good and bad.

I sound like a fat old art critic who used to be good with the ladies, and still wears his hair like he is.

You can look at a painting until you go mad, or quite easily walk by it without thinking about it for one second. He thought he knew as much about painting as anyone had before because he had seen most of the good paintings that had been painted up till his time.

'But why do you care so much about novelty, Water? You know every day is new and a new product, a brand-new shampoo, or medicine, or car is released, and who cares?' said Harriet. 'You're right.' Water replied. 'But I'll kill myself if painting is just repetition, a variation on old ideas. There must be a future with new paintings. Maybe I just can't do them.'

'You don't need to care about it. You love Renaissance or Rococo art. It's unimportant that it is not new, just that you love it and it is beautiful.'

'I don't want painting just to be some small part of culture, like contemporary poetry, or a subculture like skateboarding. They're boring. Why should I spend my whole life on a trivial activity? Perhaps it is really dead, like illuminated manuscripts or opera. Just a curiosity for snobs.'

'Thank you, Water, for your description of me as a snob,' said Harriet.

'You are, and I am a monkey on a chain dancing for the entertainment of the rich.'

Water had said similar things when he was about twelve years old, and every year since. It bored him to hear himself say them again. It was a conversation about a faith he felt forced to keep, but which was worn through and had waited too long for fulfilment. Perhaps you could say that about anything you still argued for once you got past the age of twenty-one. Even if he achieved what he talked about he might never know it. He would never admit that he was wrong, though; it was a trait that he got double from his mother and father. He had a picture in his head of his father and uncle sitting round a table arguing about nothing important, getting angrier and angrier, his uncle emotional and his father pretending to be rational. They would become incensed, losing it, unable to stop arguing, like addicts, continuing for the thrill of being themselves, and Water knew they were wrong to be like this, that it limited them, and that he was the same. His mother would give advice with certainty, and this sureness at a deeper level was different from his father's, and might have been more damaging or more beneficial. Water did not know but he was convinced nevertheless that his parents were both too sure of what they thought.

'When you're dead, darling, what will you have done?' Water asked Harriet. He was bored.

'I don't know.'

'You'll have been happy, had a nice family and career, just like everybody else but a bit better.'

'Don't be so horrible. You said you would stop doing this. If you think I am such a boring rich girl why did you want to marry me?'

'I don't. I mean I did, because I don't think you're so bad – I'm just being stupid and nasty. But tell me what do you really want to do? I'm interested.'

I didn't pretend to take her non-answer seriously.

40

Scenes from the happy marriage.

He lay in the large bath reading the *New Yorker*. Harriet pushed the door open. 'May I get in?' she asked. He put his magazine down and beckoned her with his index finger to join him. He was tired, although he had just woken up, while Harriet was enthusiastic about it being the weekend. 'You have good breasts,' he said to her. Water liked to say positive thoughts when they occurred to him. They lay there. Water picked up his magazine again but it was impossible to read it with Harriet there too. He kissed her neck and she wriggled with pleasure. She admonished him for tickling her, and then they were silent for a while. His hands rested lightly on the soft skin of her legs under the water. 'I have to wash my hair now,' she told Water. He got out of the bath, kissed her, and left the bathroom.

Scene two.

They walked into the party. Water wasn't nervous, just in a hurry to have a drink. They were celebrating/mourning the departure of Harriet's friend Soriah, who was going to Bombay to run an arts project. The guests were mostly familiar. Not good friends of his, but they knew him. He and Harriet approached Soriah to say hello. Water told her he wouldn't have this many people at his funeral, then went off to get some drinks. They were in an East London bar, which had formerly been a lap-dancing club, and had kept the pole as a feature. It was small, dark, ugly and noisy. Two friends of Soriah were on decks. Water felt that in the past Soriah had wanted to fuck him, and so he always tried to amuse her. He wondered whether Harriet noticed. She was probably just pleased he was making an effort with her friends. He didn't hide his rudeness as much as he used to. He carried the drinks through the crowd by the bar, greeting and joking with people on the way back to Harriet and Soriah. Everyone wanted to talk to Soriah, yet she was resolute in her attention to Water and Harriet. Water looked over at Soriah's boyfriend, a German photographer, who was dressed trendily but didn't seem comfortable in his clothes. He must bore her, he thought. Looks like he never did anything wrong in his life. A pretty woman with curly hair was sitting next to the boyfriend; Water caught her eye and made a silly face. She smiled. He couldn't think of anything amusing to say to Soriah and Harriet, who were deep in conversation, barely audible above the music. So he went off to say hello to Soriah's boyfriend. He wasn't so bad, and Water had a joke with him. The curly-haired woman was not introduced as she was now busy talking with what must have been her own boyfriend. Later Water got quite drunk and pretended to be a pole dancer, which everyone seemed to find funny, or at least noticed because they knew who he was.

They said goodbye to Soriah, whom Water thought was such a happy person, and he thought he must be drunk and sentimental to be thinking that, and they walked home. It wasn't far.

'Nice party, I enjoyed myself,' said Water to Harriet. He thought about Soriah, peculiar how such a warm person had had her farewell party in a bar and not at her house.

Water was awake in bed, energized by the beer he had drunk. She was almost asleep, more tired than Water from her week at work. 'I can't sleep now,' he said, kissing her. She was not enthusiastic. 'You want to sleep?' he asked her. She did and was soon unconscious. He liked having her next to him in the dark. He thought about what he would eat tomorrow, and whether Harriet would make him do something fun. Perhaps they could play tennis, or see a movie, any activity without talking would be good. It went on forever, eating, sleeping, talking, doing things, having fun. Harriet snored a little in her sleep. He laughed and closed his eyes, putting a pillow over them to block out the light sneaking through the shutters from outside. He wished he could go downstairs to watch television or masturbate, but those were not good enough reasons to wake Harriet up by clambering over her. He was imprisoned in his own bed. He wondered whether he had made a fool of himself or Harriet at the party, but decided he didn't give a fuck what those people thought, it would have been boring without him. Perhaps Harriet liked his antics. If he had been an old-fashioned painter he would have gone to his studio now to wrestle a difficult painting into a masterpiece. In those days he would not have cared about Harriet's sleep.

Scene three.

'I'm too tired to be happy today. I mean I'm tired of being happy,' said Water to Harriet.

'So would you like to be alone, unhappy in your studio?'

'You're a very considerate woman, one of the best. No, no. I'd like to be with you, just as long as we don't have to have fun.'

He looked at Harriet, his lovely wife, and wondered again why she had chosen him. She was clever, and even cleverer for not being angry at the limitations of the world.

'We could go for a walk along the Thames,' she suggested.

Water paused. 'Maybe you're right, I should be bad-tempered alone, in my studio.'

He was bored the moment he went in and smelled the oil paint. His ugly pictures made the space smaller. He called Harriet on his mobile.

'I miss you.'

'How sweet,' she said.

'What are you doing?'

'I am with Soriah. I am going to help her move some things in the car.'

'What time shall we meet?'

'What are we doing?'

'I'd like to get some Indian.'

'Phone me when you're finished in the studio.'

'OK, I will. Bye, darling.'

'Bye.'

He was finished in the studio already.

First wife, then mother. The right order.

'Hello mother (fucker).'

It was his mother on the phone; she had interrupted his dozing. Water was pleased with his motherfucker joke. His friends were shocked that he said 'fuck' to his mother. She didn't mind.

'Where are you?'

'I'm in my studio.'

'Painting?'

'Sleeping. I was reading.'

'I've done those paintings for Germany. They're not very good.' His mother had a show coming up in Düsseldorf.

'Great. I'm sure they're fine. No one will notice if they're not anyway.'

'Do you think I should do some bigger ones?'

'I wouldn't worry. They know you work small.' His mother the painter. A late period without an early one. She was quite famous now. People asked him to talk about his mother's paintings. He claimed he didn't understand them.

'I'll come now and have a look at them if you want,' he said.

'Where's Harriet?'

'She's out. I've had enough of the studio for today.'

'Where is she out?'

'With a friend. Don't worry about it. I'll leave now. See you in half an hour.'

His mother's house was messy in the way all his family's houses always were: wood floors, old furniture, books on shelves and elsewhere, and many paintings on the walls. At least four of her many dogs greeted his arrival with barking and sniffing, the rest kept their positions on sofas, chairs and in dog beds. Everywhere you looked a variation of the species was lurking, from a pair of friendly sibling caramel shit tzus to a number of hairless and hairy descendants of Monkey, their original pedigree (without the actual certificate) Chinese crested hairless.

'They stink,' said Water to his mother.

'Harry's just been sick on the sofa. He got some rotten meat out of the bin.'

'I think the smell might also be caused by the presence of nine dogs.'

'Well you can go home if you don't like it. You stop being over sensitive to it after a while,' she said. 'Dora's pregnant,' she continued.

'More puppies, fantastic. Why didn't you have her spayed? Which one is she anyway?'

'Dora is the one with hair on her head. I've put you down for one of the puppies.'

'I'll have *it* put down.'

'I see you're in a charming mood.'

'Let's just go and have a look at your paintings. Enough of this delightful small talk.'

His mother painted at her dining room table. Her new pictures showed her grandchildren in amorphous landscapes, which she said was the beach in France.

'They're quite good. They look like children discovering the sublime. Caspar David Friedrich with kids as the protagonists,' said Water, pleased with his pronouncement.

'You don't think they're too empty, not enough going on?'

'No. That's why they're good. The backgrounds are ambiguous. Everyone loves ambiguity.'

'I hope they sell one or two.'

'They'll probably sell them all. It's a good gallery.'

'That would be helpful. I need to get the roof done.'

'You could buy some more dogs. How are my sisters?'

'Louise is miserable. The other day John walked out and didn't come back for three days. Said he needed more space.'

'Where did he go?'

'He's meant to have been staying with old friends from college. Louise says it's because he hasn't had anything published for a year.'

'If he wrote better he might do.'

'Have you read any of his new stories?'

'No. I've only ever read that thing that was in the paper. It wasn't all that great.'

'Polly's painting again.'

'Great news.'

'Sarah's worried about going to New York, for her launch there. I told her to go by boat, but she says it would take too long, so every day she phones up and makes me nervous about it.'

Water's mother and sisters never changed even if their lives changed, and he stayed the same, and his father in America was always the same too. They were better than most people, which made those most people hate them, and their superiority sustained them, or at least it sustained him.

They talked and his mother served him some leftover barbecued chicken and potato salad. Then before he became grumpy he left to meet Harriet.

Not sure my mother and I have quite such flowing conversations. Neither of us listens.

He and Harriet ate Indian that night, which was boring because he had eaten too many times at the restaurant they went to.

Scene four?

41

In which I am bad. I don't care if I am immoral, amoral or just plain nasty. Harriet and Jelena are as responsible as I am for all this.

'How are you feeling? Can I send you anything?' he asked Harriet.

'No. I am fine.'

Well, she was fine and she was in the best place she could be, staying with her mother and with good doctors around if needed.

He admired her stoicism, which like her name seemed English. She was only two months pregnant. He would be there closer to the time, and would have been there now if he didn't have a show at his London gallery coming up.

'I'd better let you rest,' he said, unable to think of much else to say.

'Goodbye. Paint well.'

'Bye, darling. I send you a big kiss.'

Harriet's pregnancy had not begun well. Bleeding started while she was spending a few days in Berlin, and her doctor advised her not to travel and to avoid exertion as much as possible. Harriet's mother had had a lot of trouble conceiving and so it was expected in her family that children were not easy to produce. In Water's family new babies seemed to arrive as frequently as puppies. Water was captivated by the idea of having his own son or daughter, half his genes in circulation. Yet he knew, from his sisters, that having a family would change his life a lot, and he wondered why he had never thought more carefully about getting Harriet pregnant. Yet he had thought it inelegant to mention his doubts given that he was married to Harriet. She was very determined to be a mother before she reached thirty, and Water found no reason to argue with her logic.

His house was empty again. Soon they would be a family there: cooking, working, cleaning, talking, playing, crying, sleeping. He supposed he could afford a nanny, but he had always scorned those who subcontracted out their children's care. Now, with Harriet away, was the calm before the storm of real life began. He felt like a soldier waiting for war, or like an adolescent about to become an adult. He imagined all the decisions he and Harriet would have to take together, what time for bed and which school, and the idea of all this made him feel queasy and boyish. He reminded himself to get some flowers sent to Harriet before he went out.

He didn't miss her very often. In fact he sometimes thought he hated her, and would be glad if they never had to see each other again. Anyone whom he knew well and felt some obligation to repulsed him in time. And he wasn't good at pretending. He couldn't bear Harriet's calm efficiency, or her ability never to get angry, and knew it was ridiculous to hate nothing bad so much. He was worn out with talking to her, and even touching her. He always ran through everyone, used up his interest in them, except for his family, who exasperated him most of the time but were similar enough to himself so as to be impossible to reject.

He was meant to be painting hard for his show, but he couldn't generate the energy to concentrate on doing something new. Old ideas came back to him and they almost satisfied him. He would have to start again from scratch to recapture novelty, and he couldn't face that. Anna sent her assistant from the gallery to check his progress, which was demeaning if he thought about it too much. The assistant loved his new paintings, which looked very much like the old ones except with different subjects. Water decided he didn't give a shit if his career fucked up now, but even taking the assistant's enthusiasm at a discount, it looked likely that this show would be another staggering success. His indifference probably made him paint better, and at least there was humour in his new pictures.

The evening. On the telephone he had lied to Harriet about his plans. For no reason he had told her he was tired, so he was probably going to stay in watching television. He was actually going to the opening of a show which an old girlfriend from college was in. He had not told Harriet because it would have bored him to explain the details. She wouldn't have minded. But still, why worry her? He thought: I am the bad husband in a tacky melodrama.

The exhibition was titled 'The Figure Now' and consisted of

work by five not-very-well-known artists who painted people. Water had spent an hour reaching the gallery, which was in a side street near the Oval. It was typical – a renovated shop with wood floors and white walls, owned by a wealthy young Swiss woman with conservative taste, whose ambition seemed not to stretch much further than entertaining her London friends and selling them the odd painting. Although the gallery was packed with people, there was no one, other than Emma, he recognized. He had gone out with Emma for only a week, so still liked her in a sentimental way. When she saw him, her face clearly registered surprise that he had bothered to turn up.

'I'll get some drinks,' he said immediately. A barman had been hired to mix margaritas. Water felt like a drink, and despite having to queue for them, they were pretty good. One down and by the time he returned he already had a grin on his face.

'How do you know Emma?' her friend Esther asked.

'We made love once,' replied Water. 'How did you meet her?'

'We live together. I mean we share a flat.'

'Emma told me about you. She says you're very dirty. Disgusting. But a very nice person.' Water couldn't resist teasing.

'I'm not that untidy,' said Esther, looking to Emma for reassurance.

'Don't listen to him. Water's being a prat. He's joking.'

'Would anyone like another drink? I'll get them, to make up for my shocking insolence.' Water went off again. It wasn't too bad a crowd. He smiled at a tall pretty girl. She looked about nineteen, and she smiled back. He took a detour on his way to the bar in order to look at the paintings. Emma's were probably the best. She had a good touch. Her pictures of youths in empty rooms were quite well-painted, and there was no great reason why she had not become more successful. The rest of the work was desultory, some badly painted models done from life, a few photos that looked like substandard advertizing, a wire sculpture and two close-up paintings of heads that had been carefully copied from photographs.

The gallery owner came up to him. She said, 'Welcome. What do you think of the show?' He didn't think he had met her before, but too many cocktails had ruined his memory for acquaintances. She wasn't terrible-looking, late thirties, well dressed; he liked her Swiss accent.

'I like Emma's paintings.'

'They're very melancholic, aren't they?'

'Yes, very sad. I'm sorry, but I don't actually know your name.'

She said something that sounded like Virginia.

'My name is Nathaniel Water.'

'I know that, of course. We met a few years ago at your degree show.'

'That was about a hundred years ago, when I was young and talented.'

'I like your work very much.'

'Thanks.'

'What do you really think of the show?'

'You sure you wanna know?'

'Yes.'

'It might make you cry.'

She laughed and said she didn't mind if it did.

'It's not good enough.' He looked at her more carefully. It didn't matter if he told her the truth. She was attracted to him, and she was powerless, just an amateur pretending to be a dealer.

'Why not good enough?' she asked.

Water thought again whether he had the energy to be serious. What was the point? It was just sadism, or masochism, saying what one really thought.

'If you run a gallery you should show the best. Otherwise there is no reason to do it. Most of this work is clearly not brilliant.'

'I disagree,' she said. At that point, a male friend of hers arrived; Water excused himself, saying he had to get some drinks for his friends. He wondered why people always disagreed with the truth.

Not so evil yet. Average. Normal amount of disgust for Harriet and responsibility.

42

Let's fast forward. I don't like to go over it all. I left her, like I said I would, after she lost the baby. There was no point in continuing, when I didn't even like her that much. She didn't make too big a fuss. This is what happened to her. As usually happens, she found someone else. (Dialogue translated from the German.)

Harriet came home from work to find her boyfriend Jacob already preparing dinner. She thought he was cute. There with his wavy blond hair carefully chopping vegetables, he looked so young; he was only twenty-six.

He came over to kiss her. She felt dirty from the tram ride home, so didn't want him to, but it would have been strange to say no.

'How are you? Was your presentation a success?' he asked her.

'Yes. I think they will do it.'

'That's great. I got some wine to celebrate.' She saw that he had bought her favourite white wine.

'I'm a little tired. I will lie down for an hour before we eat. It's been a very hard day.'

'OK, you rest and I'll get on with dinner. Maybe we can just catch a movie later, if you're too tired for a party.'

'You're so sweet,' she said, hugging him. 'Now I will take my power nap.'

She went to the bedroom of their elegant small flat. It was in a good location, in a smart young area of the city. She had bought it with a loan (non-repayable) from her father, and Jacob, whom she had been seeing for a year, had helped her renovate it. He had been brilliant, very hard-working and with excellent taste. He worked part-time as an archivist in the film library at the museum. Their first encounter had been at a party there. When she walked in he had caught her eye; he was tall, handsome, and dressed well. He had noticed her too, but they had not spoken to each other that evening. By chance they met again the next day in the street, and had said hello as though they knew each other, and agreed to meet for a drink. That was the beginning much like beginnings often are: a combination of availability, coincidence and attraction.

Harriet lay in the dark, her head on the pillow, but she couldn't sleep. She thought about how nice Jacob was. He was too young, though. She wanted a man who could teach her things, and not make her feel so in control of everything. She wanted real love with a future, and marriage and a family, not as distant plans but soon. Jacob had to finish his PhD, then find a good teaching job. It would be years before he was ready to make a stable home for children. Jacob was not ready. Also she was in love with someone at the foundation (for contemporary art, where she worked as a curator). He liked her too. She hadn't even kissed him yet. It would not have been fair to Jacob. This man was in his late thirties, and was sort of her boss, although really she was responsible only to the director of the foundation. He was strong and funny, with a good job. He had spoken to her of his desire to start a family, and even said that she was the type of woman he could imagine marrying. It had been said with humour but she thought he really meant it. It was just a matter of when she told Jacob that their relationship was not working for her.

She didn't want to do what Water had done to her. She had been in hospital, and he had come to Berlin to be with her, then had left for an urgent meeting about his show and had not come back. Just phoned her and spoken with a distant voice. Then the phonecalls became less frequent. She had asked him what was wrong, and he told her he couldn't continue, and that was it. Why? She had emailed him, and he said he didn't know; it was not just him, and that's the way life was. His answer angered her. She owed it to Jacob not to do this to him. She would not tell him she had met someone else. She liked someone else because she and Jacob were not compatible in the long term, that was the real reason she wanted to end their relationship, not the man she was in love with. She and Jacob were a nice couple without a future, and she would do him the courtesy of explaining this to him gently and clearly, and she would not just say she didn't know, because you must always know. She had been in hospital and lost her baby, and then her husband had left her without even telling her why. He had said in one short letter he had written later that he could think of nothing to say to her about what had happened, that that was wrong, and made him sad. She thought that maybe he had already started seeing Jelena again, or that he had never stopped with her. It was unfair that she was left with all this doubt, jealousy and anger. He would probably do the same thing to Jelena that he had done to her. Yet she didn't really want another person to suffer as she had. How could your husband, who was married to you, who had said he loved you, who had written you long love letters, just leave you because he had run out of conversation, when you had just got out of hospital, and you were as sad as you had ever been? Water was an egotist, she thought, and perhaps a sadist. Maybe he took pleasure in destroying women, one by one, as retribution for growing up in a family of women. Maybe he had stopped loving her because she had failed to give him a child. She would not leave Jacob with such doubt. She felt like crying. She had never cried much before, but Water had broken some of her dreams and faith in the future. She was tempted to read Water's last letter to her, to confirm that it had all really happened, but she resisted the urge, and decided to get up, to eat a nice dinner with her boyfriend whom she would soon be leaving.

Yes.

43

Jelena's back. And gone. Far. Christmas again! Again? Again!

Water looked round his house. It was bigger now he was alone. The mess didn't seem so bad when there was no one else to blame. Jelena's black bra, which he had given her, lay on the chest in his bedroom. The double bed was missing most of the pillows. He could do what he wanted. She had discarded the bra to send him a message. Perhaps she was marking her territory. He went into the small room next door. Because she wouldn't stop complaining, he had slept there in the single bed most nights she had been in his house. His double bed, which she had forced him out of, would smell of her for the first night after she left, then would return to normal. He would have to wash the duvet cover sometime. He felt he would miss the small room; it had nice light, and it was good moving rooms in your own house – like a holiday. His stomach ached from the overeating of the previous days. One afternoon he had been enchanted by the carpet of broken glass covering his wood floors, which she had made by smashing most of his wine glasses. He had been angry at her leaving the bathmat soaked in the water she had splashed over the bath's edge, angry that she always flooded the floor, angry that if he mentioned it she flew off the handle. He thought what he had said often: you're alone, you're always alone. Her visit had finished without unpleasantness. They spent the last day and a half in harmony. Once they knew there was only a short time left it was easier to control themselves.

'It's difficult for two people to live together.' 'We don't really like being together so let's stop pretending; this love is a fantasy.' 'We don't have to stay together.' Water stated the obvious to Jelena. His mother said she liked Jelena, and that made him suspicious.

Whenever he split up with a girlfriend, Water's mother would tell him he reminded her of her cousin's first husband, John Foreman.

'These girls always believe it's going to last forever. And then you get bored and leave them. John Foreman was the same.'

Water protested. 'What am I meant to be, nasty from the start?'

His mother replied, 'All the presents and flowers you give them, you pursue them, and they think it's real.'

'I like to do things in style. Anyway it's not my fault things don't last. They're not victims, with me as the bad man messing them around.' He knew he was saying too much; his mother would take it as confirmation that she was right.

'I like Jelena,' she said.

'So do I. Listen, it's none of your business anyway,' he said, trying to escape.

His mother's words remained in his head. Her confidence in her insights into his character annoyed him; they seemed to foretell a future repeating the present. Water didn't want his mother believing that he had failed with Jelena too. He didn't even want her cunning ideas circulating in his thoughts. But perhaps she was right.

Along his ugly road they had walked, never counting all the dirty bricks that made the Victorian houses.

'Look how beautiful this is,' he told Jelena. 'The Portuguese are in their café, always celebrating. The shops are open late, and you can buy the best bread in London here. The sky is amazing above the houses. Life is here. It's not boring like Rome.' Jelena was angry because a moment before he had told her to shut up and stop moaning, as they had marched along the dark street in the drizzle.

She had spent Christmas with his family. Buying presents had been her biggest worry. That his family would laugh at what she gave them. 'I don't care, I hate Christmas,' he told her nearly every day. There had been no tree in his house. So many sisters and children to find gifts for, but finally it was fun, different from her small family. That was the difference between them, he being the youngest with so many sisters and she an only child. In Slovakia Christmas was mainly Christmas Eve. There he had gone to a Christmas Eve service with her and felt false in the crowd filling the large Lutheran church. In London on Christmas Eve he made a nice dinner and they watched TV. Christmas Day, God he even hated the words and their endless merry repetition. It hadn't been so bad. His big family opened vast numbers of presents, so many that a few were lost when the wrapping paper was binned. Jelena was pleased with what she had received, and his family wasn't rude about what she had given them. Then there was nothing to do until dinner. A few hours of sitting, asking when it would be ready, and finally it was consumed quickly with a few jokes and Christmas crackers. And then time to go home. All novel for Jelena, unreal and inescapable in its repetition for Water. But Christmas Day had made them happy and that night they had slept together for the first time in a week.

New Year's Eve. What was he doing? Watching TV with his new shoes on. She? An hour ahead, finished off a duck for dinner. His voice echoed back to him on the phone as they talked long distance lightheartedly. It sounded so smug, semi-upper-class drawl and a little American, a voice of a chuckling man in love with himself. After the storm always calm, but more and more wary or weary. Jelena said she didn't know if she was pregnant. Water often asked her why she wanted to be. He could not even conceive of it really happening, let alone desire or fear it, but supposed with a gambler's fatalism that it might. He would deal with the consequences then. It was so important for her in her small family. He asked her what she was thinking. She spoke. He said, 'It's hard to be happy in the present.'

'I am.'

'Not with me.'

'I was sometimes.'

'Not alone with me.'

'When we were walking along the river. I am happy when you're not.'

He remembered she had been, but he had been still angry with her, and had thought she was pretending, or had not been able to adjust quickly enough to be in sync. He had walked along the south bank of the Thames often, so was bored with the view. A New Year. Everybody kept asking what he was doing for it. The usually gregarious Water was hibernating and would not be going out. Nothing was wrong, he just wanted a lot of time to think. There could never be enough time to sleep, dream, watch television and think. He hardly left the house, just a walk once a day to buy a loaf of bread, or not even that. No newspaper, because that was too much of the world and would tell him what day it was in a way the TV wouldn't. He was doing nothing for New Year. What had it done for him? He was quite rich and well-known, and owned a house, and had had many pretty girlfriends. And another year probably wasn't going to change that. On the TV a million people had been around Sydney harbour, and one hundred thousand Hogmanayed in Edinburgh. It all looked better on television. He had been in Rome for the Millennium, and it was quite boring after five minutes being in a big crowd with fireworks in the sky, and nothing to do, really.

Maybe he should call Jelena, an hour ahead. After that he could relax until his own New Year. One of his friends had asked what he was going to do and Water had told him watch a porn film and his friend had asked him which one and Water had had no answer. In the next year he hoped life would be more distinct. Certain romantically optimistic notions of a good life were in his head but he could not bring himself to bring them into focus and find out exactly what they were. Just phone Jelena and see what happens. This year will be over then, and you can relax and get on with the new one, he thought. To himself, obviously.

She told me she knew I would come back to her. That she was the best, and that I would know that when I grew up, and stopped with German whores. She was right, although Harriet wasn't a whore, but that's just one of Jelena's charming expressions. I always liked that she believed in our inevitability.

Less than a year till next Christmas.

44

This is ridiculous, like real life is. Divorce from Harriet took six months (six months from the point when we were allowed to get divorced; you have to wait twelve months from when you are married to start divorce proceedings!), boring forms to fill in, no financial settlement, no paying her forever because the marriage was short, we both had careers, no children, and she was reasonable. I sound like I'm fifty years old, like an old bitter guy in a pub talking about his life. I was not even thirty. I could marry pregnant Jelena.

He lay in the grass and a big cloud blocked out the weak English sun. So what that it was nearly summer, it would still rain most days. He needed to make the most of even a little warmth. But he was in sandals and a T-shirt, having walked out of the house to avoid her hitting him anymore, more accurately to avoid hitting her back hard, or watching her smash up the TV or other valuable items. She had thrown a glass from the sitting room onto the tiles of the kitchen floor. She was six months pregnant, so it wasn't a good time for violent arguments. Also, she had only broken one glass tumbler, not half a set of bowls and most of the wine glasses, like he remembered her doing before. Pregnancy had made her calmer and she ate more reasonably, too.

The field near his house was full of clean grass, and big enough that he could experience some serenity/silence. He wondered where all the dog shit and piss went. Probably the dogs preferred to use the long grass, or perhaps the rain washed it nutritiously into the soil. He lay down on the grass. For a moment the sun appeared, and it felt like his skin was being tanned. Then after a few moments of joy, the clouds moved and he was cold again. Jelena was going be his wife, he was going to be a father, this woman who was Jelena would be the mother of his child. He was marrying a woman he hated, and they would spend the rest of their life arguing over their daughter (against his wishes she had found out the sex of the baby). It wasn't as bad as that, for if he truly hated her why would he marry her? He must have loved or now love her, in a way different from his previous girlfriends. For God's sake, he had been married once, and he had been engaged to Jelena before: he should know what he was doing.

Circumstances, and the order of events, might explain the peculiar situation. It was not as though he had no experience of unsuccessful marriages besides his own. His parents were an example. But how could he criticize the union on which his existence was predicated?

He and the world, the people he knew, like Jelena, were attached to each other with rope. A coarse rope that burnt the hands of those who tried to hold onto it. When others were happy, he was melancholy; their concerns would seem to him meaningless and depressingly trivial. If his friends had problems, when they cried, or Jelena cried, he was happy, relentlessly optimistic, helpful and full of good advice. He always said 'a bad mood shared is a bad mood lost', but the problem was more serious than that; there was not enough rope for everyone, and so the tension, the pulling back and forth, would never end.

Jelena demanded reassurance, though she wouldn't ask for it directly.

'Give me some more orange juice.'

'No, make it yourself. I'm drinking this.'

'Come with me to the park.'

'Which park? I'll only go to the one near the house.'

'You bought the milk I can't drink. It makes me sick.'

'Don't drink it then.'

'I'll be there at seven.'

'It starts at six-thirty.'

'You are destroying my life.'

'I have always been the same. I don't understand why you chose me if I am so bad.'

'Wake up.'

'No.'

'You're lazy.'

'I don't wake *you* up.'

On an Italian island he had loved a woman in a bikini. She was Jelena. But it couldn't have been a bikini, because she had refused to wear the bikini he had given her. The bronze sun had shone on the beach, and after they had argued or sulked all day, he had carried her up one hundred stairs, up from the beach to their house. Then he had nearly vomited a stomach full of wine and grappa. She must have been the same then and it frightened him that memory might even idealize what was happening now. There was consolation in memory and none in that things were continuous, always the same. He read only sad books at this time, in the present, of cancer wards and gulags, because those stories made him count his blessings.

He was lying on the sofa, and the room was a zoo. A mosquito had been pestering him for the last twenty pages. It was a fat slow one but still he couldn't kill it. A big spider was trying to escape from the bathtub and would probably be joining the party soon. A daddy longlegs was dancing round the unshaded bulb. There were flies and ants too. A moth might arrive any moment. Life was drawn to the light on a hot night with the window open. The cat (not his, for he had no cat) was outside on the roof again. Sometimes when the garden door was open it would steal into his house to look for mice or other food. The book was climaxing with no happy endings, just more cancer for all, including the doctors. It was sad in a beautiful way. When he had finished it, he read the blurb on the back and realized he had missed the central metaphor, so obvious was it. He had been more interested in whether the heroic patient would end up with the right woman. Love stories are more appealing than metaphors, he thought, and they are what keep you reading.

Remember when Jelena looked through all the photos of Water's old girlfriends? She wasn't jealous so Water fell in love with her. Now when she stayed in his house it was different. Jelena's mother was in the spare bedroom. She didn't speak English but you didn't need it to understand the rage and swearing of their arguments. It was a foreign movie for her, unreliably translated.

An odd tale where out of nowhere, say a situation of waiting at a bus stop – all could change in seconds: the young lovers are talking; Jelena asks Water something; he replies; she talks some more; he becomes angry, pointing and scolding; she starts shouting; he says ugly words and walks off; she begins screaming and crying. One morning, Jelena asks Water to show her mother some photos of when he was a child. That's fine, but then she wants the photos of his old girlfriends. Water says no. She digs through his stuff anyway, and shows them to her mother. Jelena enraged, her mother puzzled, Water with temper frayed, another day destroyed.

Overall it was better to have Jelena's mother with them for the two weeks before the wedding. She and Jelena would also fly back to Slovakia together, so it would be a peculiar honeymoon, Jelena and her mother travelling home and Water going with his friends to Venice. Jelena was six months pregnant and it was Water's second marriage and she was Water's second pregnant wife. The story of him and his many sisters and their parents' broken marriage he was fast and helplessly remaking with a few new twists. History repeated as farce. Still, not to worry, he had never vowed to be any different from his parents. He had just wanted to be a good artist, and that goal was timeless, and whatever else happened was irrelevant gossip. Jelena's mother was another outlet for Jelena's overflowing need for love, constant, unceasing, uncritical love, the kind of love which Water was empty of, had never contained even, for he was just an efficient hunter and had only seemed like what she needed. Water had got more than he bargained for, but it didn't matter.

The baby clothes on the sofa were from the cheap Turkish supermarket near his house. Water gathered from the conversation between Jelena and her mother that they were discussing baby clothes. He thought Jelena might be saying that she would take a bus to Rome to pick up some old ones that her friend and ex-employer, a rich gallerist, had offered to her. Baby clothes. Second-hand, as if Water could not or would not provide them, or at least the money to buy them. Such absurdity was the worthless currency of their relationship now. Water didn't even argue that often. He had switched to zero patience (the sudden walk-off as she was in mid-flow) and occasional surprise counterattacks (withholding something she wanted as punishment for a grudge he bore from the day before). They had been at his mother's house for dinner that evening. He had hardly spoken; Jelena had been half an hour late for no reason, angry about something. Water played with the new puppies, the third generation of mongrel Chinese cresteds that his mother enjoyed. They were funny dogs with flat faces from the their shit tzu father and the hairlessness and grey skin of their mother. One of them had patches of wiry orange hair on its head and back. It was a lovable orangutan, a novelty at least. Water liked this dog as he had not liked a dog for a long time, the words describing it sounding peculiar and contrived, but the dog was good. Too many dogs in his family, many bad dogs, or badly behaved dogs, and he was catching the sickness, wanting one for himself. Owning a dog: vaccinations, holidays more difficult, dog passports and microchips, a stinking house. And then it would need a friend, another dog; soon he would have thirteen dogs like his mother. The madness of it. A dog was nearly as much work as a baby.

He thought, I am teaching her to hate me, and there's no helping it, as he hung up on her for the third time. You cannot teach people anything; you cannot change them. Maybe you can, but the effort of reverse psychology, of deception, is too great to be worth it. She will either decide to improve or not. She may hate my didactic, critical nature, but at least I am happy in a self-contained way. I can read, or paint, or watch TV, or eat dinner, and I require

no other person to help me enjoy those experiences. It's not even that. I know that if she behaved (what an awful word) normally for a while, then I'd probably still find reasons to dislike her. Her unreasonable moaning, anger and destruction of moments. Her demanding selfish nature. Her total lack of perception of others' desires, needs or wants. Her editing of all that I say, to remember only the insults, the blows to her esteem. She who does nothing, and demands everything. Yet his mother, his sisters, her family, his father, men, some women, most children. They liked her. She was pretty, but it must have been the contrariness of human nature. Or perhaps she wanted to be loved and so they loved her.

Water took Jelena and her mother to dinner at a Pakistani restaurant he had been to many times because it was cheap, quick, served lots of grilled meats and was superior to most other Indian (subcontinental) restaurants. It was on a street with a mosque and a synagogue, near the hospital and next to an abandoned mental asylum. Across from the restaurant there was a house for sale, and Water took down the number on the 'for sale' board, thinking that this would be a nice place to live. They were crammed around a table, in the conservatory section, which was more like a sheltered alleyway. Water had spent the afternoon playing tennis with a friend, while Jelena and her mother had been shopping on

Oxford Street. They had arrived laden with bags from shops that Water rarely went to because they were not expensive enough. In his mind, quality and cost were usually proportionally related, except in restaurants.

Jelena ate lots of the very piquant food, while her mother was more circumspect with this cuisine that was new to her. He didn't feel that hungry; perhaps exercise had killed his appetite. The food didn't taste that good to him. The mix of spices was jarring, and Jelena's mother asked him why he wasn't eating. The enjoyment of eating at this restaurant had faded, was near to gone, through repetition or maybe because the cooking had just got worse. The *nans* were stale, he thought, remembering that he had said before that their *nans* were better than the best pizza in Rome.

Afterwards he took them to a new bar on Brick Lane. 'This area is where everyone goes out,' he found himself saying. Who was this everyone? 'The Indian [subcontinental] restaurants here are mostly really bad, just tourist places. You get a few bits of meat floating in an oily sauce.'

Jelena's mother was in a good mood, appreciative of these moments of peace between her daughter and future son-in-law. For some reason, thought Water, Jelena is not in a bad mood. The bar was trying to be stylish, with different textures, lighting effects and islands of square sofas. They talked about nothing – that London was less expensive than her mother had expected, that it was efficient, that the shops were better than Rome. Then Water said he thought there was much more life in London than in Rome, and they got into an argument because he said he liked that you could be alone in London. And Jelena said he didn't know what it meant, to be isolated, and he said he hadn't meant that, and she said she was really isolated being pregnant in London, coming from her country. And Water said that wasn't really the point. Anyway, she was here with her mother (and him).

And Jelena got angry, and Water asked her why she was always so aggressive. Then her mother changed the subject and they went home on the tube quite content.

He thought, this tension is what I want to describe. The contorted look on her face. Nothing will work; it's all going to be difficult. Only problems. There are traps all over the place. Next minute she'll be screaming and attacking me with her fists. Her mother and me, and my friend and her, in this room. We're all powerless to stop the disaster. Next week we'll be married and in three months there'll be a child too, a little hostage. Already the end point of each argument is 'I am pregnant'. That is the be-all and end-all. As though she was any better before she was pregnant. The anger makes you a little nervous in the stomach. The shouting makes your hair grey. Life gives you bleeding haemorrhoids. It is repetition and always tension with her. Either the storm, or when the storm is electricity or pressure in the air, or when it is sunny knowing it won't last, that it could start again because of a poor choice of conversation. And why do we put up with this? Because one of us is her mother. Because I am her future husband who loves her. My innocent friend is just here to borrow a camera. He has nothing to lose, and I suppose he envies us, thought Water. I am not so wonderful myself, but she makes me forget this, too busy hating her.

In the end Water planned the wedding. He wondered why he had ended up with two brides whose families couldn't organize weddings. He paid for it himself too, because he had money, and he who pays the piper calls the tune.

45

The night before Christmas. No. The night before my second wedding. I wonder if someone had said you don't have to do this, I would have listened to their advice, and not done it. If wishes were horses, French people would eat them. Gallows humour. Unfunny. I laugh.

'It's your last night of freedom,' said his mother to him as he walked away from the car at two o'clock in the afternoon.

Of all the stupid things to say, so many stupid people had said it to him, and now his mother. She was the only one who might convince him that the words had meaning. Water, as though his mother were still the programmer of his actions, phoned his friend Joshua and told him they had to go out because it was his stag night. Joshua, having recently split up with his girlfriend of eight years, should have been perfect for the occasion, but he had just met a new girl, though he said it would be fun if they all met up.

At 4.30pm Water took a taxi to the casino in Tottenham Court Road. Before he began drinking he felt like gambling. He loved the rush of crowds in the centre of London, and then entering the calm madness of the casino. The cards, roulette wheels, gamblers (all losers) and dealers (all cynics). He liked sitting drinking a Coke with ice, eating a ham and tomato sandwich from the little table placed next to the big card table. He would try to double his money, sometimes losing a thousand or so, often succeeding in winning a few hundred. He knew how to play blackjack, but knew these games – unless you had an edge (and no one did) – were unwinnable. He assumed, because he knew all this, that he just played for the pleasure of oblivion, of concentration on how much he was up or down each shoe, of the thrill of having lost too much money, and his desire to make money effortlessly (though actually it was quite hard work sometimes, sitting there playing cards when you were bored, tired or drunk). The compulsion was the same as those of others who enjoy what seems pointless.

Gamblering. Jelena calls it that. At least it pisses her and everyone else off. Nothing they can't stand like wasting money. Don't talk about it; it's time made as meaningless as when you have a headache.

Joshua phoned him around six-thirty, to see if he was on his way. No mobiles at the table, the dealer reminded him, and Water felt disgruntled to break from the blackjack. Still, he would go soon, no matter what. He was playing steadily. Having lost his initial two hundred pounds, he had started playing fifty pounds a hand, and now he was two hundred up, but he would have liked a little more. Everyone, from the mouthy white guys to the Chinese students to the old Greek men, clicked, shuffled rattled or fondled their chips near constantly. The casino's TV was on too loud, so you could hear it, and they were piping in a love song over the top. Water felt wonderfully happy and sang along to it, the words just breaking out from under his breath. The pit boss looked surprised to see such a happy gambler.

He went out the door four hundred pounds up at seven o'clock in the evening with the light still bright. He took a taxi to the bar, chatting with the driver about who would win the Derby the next day, and he tipped him a fiver and The Great Gatsby (which came second at 16-1).

Tough guy.

'Hi, Joshua. I won,' said Water, full of exuberance.

'This is Sabien.'

'How d'you do. Good to meet you,' said Water. Joshua always went for these pretty European students. Sabien seemed quite shy but with reasonable English.

'Let's go get drunk. There's an opening down the road.'

Joshua looked at Sabien as if to say 'this is what I told you about.'

'You have to understand that Water is a real man about town!'

'We both used to be quite unsuccessful bachelors. Do you like art, Sabien?'

The three of them ploughed into the opening at around 8pm. Drinking mini-bottles of champagne they watched French performance artists play with a giant ball made of soft felt. It was quite a pretty sight in the street outside the gallery, the ball bouncing on a parked Mercedes and rising in the dusky sky. Water grabbed the ball and threw it at Joshua and Sabien; it bounced harmlessly off them. He drank more champagne, ignoring the headache it gave him. A woman was hit on the head by the slow sphere and she, with her face contorted into grumpiness, told the artists to be more careful. Water went to talk to a woman who seemed to be one of the artists.

'Why do you throw this ball around?'

'It creates a situation,' she replied.

'Everything is a situation.'

His mobile rang.

'I'm sorry.' It was a friend confirming, a little late, that he and his wife would be attending the ceremony the next day.

'So I was saying, what's the reason you create this situation?' he said.

'Well you know, it's not a usual situation.'

Her phone rang and she took the call without apologizing. She was French and pretty, her prettiness enhanced by a large birthmark across her neck. He noticed such noticeable things, but they made little impression on him; they didn't matter anymore.

'Listen, we have to meet some friends for a drink. It's just up the road. Why don't you come there later and we can make a situation.'

She said it sounded nice. She would see if her friends wanted to.

Joshua grinned at him as they walked to the bar.

The bar was filled with those who didn't know who he was. They had boring jobs so liked to be part of the East End nightlife.

They were bad actors, unable to conceal their conformity. They are no worse than I am, he thought. I want to be part of the big club of bohemian genius artists. They want to be here. Joshua's girlfriend was drunk, quite funny with her silly accent. Water wondered if she would rather sleep with him than Joshua.

'Hello there, Mr Rude!' A short woman greeted him as he wandered though the bar.

'Hello Miz Rude,' said Water, before he recognized her as the barmaid from the opening, who had objected to him taking three mini-bottles of champagne at a time.

'I'll get you a drink,' he said, 'and one for your friend.'

He reflected how rudeness always indicated attraction; perhaps the worst thing was to meet someone who seemed to like you.

'It's my stag night. You can be the stripper if you like,' he said to her.

'What a charming offer,' she replied.

'I don't actually know your name.'

'Do you want to?' On it went. He hardly found her attractive, but flirtation seemed the natural course to take.

'Are you a virgin?' A question that he would be embarrassed by when he remembered it.

'Why does it matter?'

'I'd like to sleep with a virgin on my wedding eve.'

'And that would be me, would it? You think I'd do that?'

'I think you might. I think you quite like me, and therefore it's possible, or you wouldn't be talking to me now.'

'You're quite perceptive.' He hated all the quites in the world.

'Let's go now. I'll take you to a hotel next to here.'

'I would prefer to sleep with you after you're married.'

'Rubbish. You're just making excuses because you're scared.'

'Maybe.'

'Are you really a virgin?'

'Nearly. I've slept with three men.'

'Hmm. That's an interesting number.'

They danced for a while. He threw his arms out in the air, and bent his knees, and wobbled them too. He had reached the stage where he enjoyed dancing. They danced close to each other, and their bodies touched, rubbing front to back, but she was too short for him, and not a virgin. Their dancing didn't seem that elegant.

He said he was going to the toilet, and left without goodbyes, down the fire escape staircase, and out onto the warm busy street. A minicab was there, and the driver agreed to take him home for a tenner. As Water sank back in the car seat he looked at the time on his mobile phone. It was 12.06 and today he was getting married.

46

Married again. Lots of fun.

The day after they got married he slapped her in the face in front of her mother and her best friend. His friends said it was the best wedding they had ever been to. Of course it was, that was what he had planned. He knew what he was doing even if sometimes he could make the stupidest of mistakes. She grabbed him by his favourite shirt and wouldn't let go, taunting him to kick her in her pregnant stomach. He wriggled free, by ripping himself out of his shirt. He was there in front of her, and them, bare-chested, and seeing that she had destroyed another thing he liked, he was angry, hating her, so he slapped her calmly, without force, in the face, and walked out of his house.

He was to blame this time, for he had provoked her to attack him. That morning, the day after the ceremony and the day of the party, in his nasty quiet voice, he had told her that she was stingy because she and her ungrateful family had paid nothing towards the wedding. He had told her that she was a horrible selfish bitch who expected to be treated like a princess but gave nothing and therefore should expect nothing from him. He had gone on until she had attacked him. Being hateful to her was more pleasurable than being nice, because then at least he got what he deserved.

I extended it over two days. Drew it out. Ceremony Saturday. Party Sunday. Say everything three times, in case they don't get it the first two.

Water was not pleased with his wedding presents. The worst things he received were an electric spa footbath and a set of castanets. The day Jelena left to go back to Slovakia with her mother, he told her that he was very happy to be rid of her, her mother and her stinking friends and that she and her mother could pay for their own taxi to the airport with the money they had saved on the wedding. He didn't care what she wanted because she was a bloody bitch. He shut the glass door, to separate him from her, as she screamed. So she threw a vase, one of the better wedding gifts, at the door. The heavy vase cracked the safety glass into quite a pretty spider's-web pattern. He didn't return to his house until she and her mother had left.

He didn't dance with Jelena at the party. Her mother kept telling him to tell Jelena she looked beautiful, which she did, but Water didn't want to say it. When they cut the cake he pretended to stab her with the knife. The happy crowd around them shouted for them to kiss, which they did: he moved his lips near her mouth, then brushed her cheek with them. The DJ played his repetitive beats in the kitchen, and there were candles in the garden, and his house was fuller with people than it ever had been. It was a beautiful party. The music only stopped when the amplifier burnt out. At the end he challenged her Italian friends to a football match against his friends. Just before sunrise they climbed railings and ran about in the dark of the park near his house, and they shouted, fell over and laughed. The Italians won 7–2. That night he didn't speak one word to her except necessary things like 'pass me that cup please' or 'excuse me, I need to get past.' After she went home, he took all the cards of congratulation and threw them in the big rubbish bin outside. He had intended to write thank you letters, but she had opened all the presents, and it was confusing to work out exactly who had given what. Anyway, it seemed an old-fashioned practice, and he couldn't be bothered being grateful for a bunch of junk. She told him afterwards that it had been a good wedding, which it had been. He took a long time to get the glass door repaired, and he made little effort to collect the wedding photos which his friend had taken. People asked if he wanted copies of their photos, but he told them he preferred to just remember it all, and that he never looked at photos.

'You must both learn to compromise,' Jelena's friend said to him. She had stayed a day longer than Jelena.

'Yes, you're right.' Water looked at this woman, who was advising him on how to make his two-day-old marriage work.

'You are both very strong people,' she carried on.

'I know.'

'She was very frightened when she was pregnant in Rome and you didn't come to see her.'

Water felt himself being drawn in.

'I wanted to come, but then she made problems, so I didn't,' he said.

'When a woman is pregnant she is very vulnerable, she has many feelings. It is very major change, physically and emotionally.'

'Yes, probably sometimes I underestimate that, but Jelena was always like she is.'

'You both want to be in control. I think that you have difficulty expressing what you feel, yet all this, your relationship, certainly must come from a strong love you have for each other.'

'I understand that, but Jelena has not got used to the idea that there are other people in the world who have the same fears and needs as she does. She has no awareness that anyone else exists. She's an only child. I come from a large family. So maybe she never learned that.'

'It is so interesting to hear you. Both sides of the story are very different. And neither is untrue.'

'Yes.'

'This is an important time, before the baby is born. Maybe you could write to her. She needs to know that you support her. With letters, or emails, there is no argument. You have time to say what you want. It would be more calm than when you are together.'

'I will write to her,' said Water. He looked at the shattered glass door, and wished Jelena's friend would go away. Even her crappily obvious advice made him feel like crying.

47

Honey moon.

After he was married he went to the Venice Biennale on his honeymoon, which was the scene of his earlier glory. This was solipsistic enough, but worse was that his bride, the lovely Jelena, did not accompany him. She had a pregnancy checkup scheduled, for which she returned to Slovakia with her mother, two days after the wedding.

Got it? She left me. I'm not so bad, you see. Can all this have happened so quickly? It's possible. I'm in a rush; no time to lose before death.

Friends asked, 'Where are you two going to live?' Water replied that he didn't know, he took one day at a time. Jelena answered that Water did not want her (and their child) to live with him.

Water went to Venice with a couple of friends instead of Jelena. He thought it might have been good to go alone, but it was nice to have a permanent audience around, even if sometimes the performance got a bit tiring. He was ecstatic in Venice. The sunshine was thirty-six degrees Celsius, and the sweating heat made him very happy. Each time he had been there he had been happy. The memories overlaid each other without guilt. This was where he had betrayed Harriet; this was where he'd walked away from Jelena; this had been his Biennale; this was where he would honeymoon without his wife Jelena. It was all golden and beautiful, and could not be destroyed by all the tourists in the world.

In Venice acquaintances were everywhere, congratulating him on his wedding; he searched for people who did not know him, so as to be anonymous in doing what he wanted. He could even feel his two friends (whose hotel bills he was subsidizing) watching him, as if noting down his actions for future anecdotes. People wanted to talk to him less than they had, he had gone from the nicest and most obliging of young artists to become a difficult man who spoke his mind, but all his success insulated him from much disapproval: he could be categorized amongst the powerful and slightly eccentric.

Just married and looking to pick up women, what an idea. Water said to himself that he should have sex on his honeymoon. It was indeterminate whether he intended to sleep with the women he propositioned, or whether he just enjoyed the pursuit without need of the quarry. It seemed like he would just see what happened.

'Hello. What's your name?' It was what Water thought Joey on *Friends* said as his pickup line.

'My name is Eliane. What's yours?'

'Nathaniel Water.'

'How very English,' she said, in a quite good mock-English accent.

'Where are you from? Not England. Perhaps Holland?'

'Guess again.'

'Nordic areas? I don't know. Tell me!'

'Belgium,' she said.

In the dark of the garden she laughed with intelligence. He had shaken off his friends, who had fallen in with a gang of Welsh women. But he was surely being observed by someone who knew him. What was wrong with him talking to people? They were at a party, of course, at a show in a hotel that had never been completed, and he was one of those many ugly cheating men from history who had been unable to control themselves – those big egos who wanted to dominate another pretty woman just to prove they could. And they never got bored with the same pickups; their genius did not stretch that far.

'I'm on my honeymoon.' Moon, honey.

'Congratulations. Where is your wife?' she replied.

'Oh, she had a medical appointment in Slovakia. She's from Slovakia. I am here with two friends. It's a contemporary honeymoon,' he explained. 'Do you have a husband?'

'No. I am single.' This she said in a way he thought significant.

They talked some more. He asked her questions which made him seem interested in her life. He said enigmatic things about himself. Later she told him she had never considered him as a potential sexual partner once he had said he was married (or perhaps even before that). What she said seemed reasonable, but Water didn't believe her, women often denied they saw situations sexually. Women, Water thought, talked about men's talents and goodness, instead of just reducing them to the possibility of sex, which must at some level have occurred to them. Men believed women to be interesting, and women thought men to be good for the same reason: the hope of love, intimacy, sex or other.

Profound.

The pursuit of Eliane began that night. The prerequisites were minimal: she was pretty; she had said with emphasis that she was single; and she resisted him but gave him her phone number.

The next day they met by accident. (Water had calculated the probabilities and arranged to be in the place where he had the most chance of bumping into her.)

'Hi, it's you again,' she said.

He was tired from the previous night, and didn't have much energy to be witty.

'Let's meet for a drink later,' he said, getting straight to the point and hoping to arrange a meeting out of the glare of others' sight (which was almost impossible in Venice).

'OK, where?' She still seemed naïve (or to be feigning naïvety) about his purpose.

'We can meet at the bar here around six-thirty.' A stupid suggestion, for the bar was right next to the national pavilions and always packed full of his acquaintances, but he didn't know the names of any other bars.

Fortunately she didn't show up. He was left drinking with a whole group of friends – his Berlin gallerist and some artists from London. It was a nightmare waiting for her, hoping she would come, not sure how to introduce her if she did. 'This is a girl I picked up last night.' 'Yes my wife's fine; the baby's due next month.' He liked honesty, especially in his imagination.

He phoned her as soon as he got a moment to himself. The repetition! Now he wanted her more because she was difficult to get. The need to conquer, the sin which he always fell into. He never learned. She said she had lost his card with his phone number on it. She had been tired and gone home for a shower. Yes, she would like to go to the British party that night. Water thought: it's a risk taking her there, but so audacious no one would suspect that he was trying to sleep with her. They knew he had just got married. He could pull it off. The key to lying was to realize how little people knew of your desires.

The party was a disappointment, of course. He was nervous and drank too much. She arrived late with her stolid friend. Water suggested they all go swimming. They could take a boat up to the Lido. Water remembered swimming at night with some girls in South Africa. The next day, sober, they had told him about the sharks. But it was a beautiful memory of being in the warm Indian Ocean, holding hands (that must have been to protect against the sharks) in the night with the stars clear above. At first Eliane seemed willing, but her friend was tired. They had a long drive the next day back to Antwerp. He cajoled them, but it was a losing battle. Why was the archetypal friend always tired, and why did her lack of desire always win out? The friend was no friend. She was protection. So all of a sudden Water gave up convincing them, her and her unyielding friend, and said goodnight, it was a great pleasure to meet you, perhaps we'll meet again in a Flanders field, and he walked off. Of course he knew he'd phone Eliane or write her a witty email the day after he was back in London. He couldn't stop or leave alone what he had started. It would have been better if he and Eliane had had sex that night. Then it would have been finished and he wouldn't have liked her anymore, or at least not for long.

There were a few more parties which weren't that much fun. Then the hours before the plane home. His friends were on a different flight, fortunately. He woke up very early, the heat enlivening him, pushing him out onto the street. No more contemporary art. He had missed a lot of the Biennale. There was nothing good to see. This art world he was king of (or at least one of its princes) was very empty, which made him love it, power over

real things of value or use that moved people's lives was boring in its simplicity. Art which did not exist, or so rarely that you could hardly believe in it, was worth pursuing. Before he left Venice, he went to the Accademia gallery and looked at Veronese's *Dinner at the House of Levi*, an enormous painting (perhaps thirty feet wide), *Last Supper* style.

It was still good to look at. He left Venice happy, the sun shining, that good painting in his head, and Eliane a possibility.

The family again. My nephew's birthday.

They ate lunch together to celebrate the birthday of Polly's son Felix. They were all there, his family of women: mother and four sisters. His wife, pregnant with his daughter, was in Slovakia. Water's father, although visiting England at that time, was not there because Water and his sisters were not speaking to him. The dispute was, as usual, about money, which was a more concrete thing to be angry about than feelings, and thus caused the worst problems. There were Polly's three children, Frances's two boys and Sarah's son. Sarah and Frances's boyfriends were there. Polly's was not, they had split up. Louise's boyfriend was there but silent. What a lineup!

My sisters' lives change: a boyfriend goes, then returns. Doesn't much matter. My mum phones to tell me the news.

Water arrived late at the organic pub. He had been early – at another pub, the organic pub's non-organic mirror image – and sat down with a Coke and a newspaper to wait for the rest of the family. The organic pub was as it should be, crammed full of out-of-control children and parents discussing which were the best local schools.

'I think I'll just have some fizzy water. I ate before we came,' said his mother surveying the chalkboard menu. Her lips expressed that she wouldn't or couldn't eat anything that was there.

'Do you have chips?' Polly asked the waitress.

'We only have what's on the board. There are boiled potatoes.'

'The children can't eat any of that stuff,' said Polly to Sarah. Water was glad that he hadn't chosen this place. Sarah, who had, looked like she was about to cry.

'Now you know what it's like being with Jelena,' said Water. 'She never likes anywhere we go.'

'I thought there'd at least be chips for the children,' said Polly.

'Couldn't you have the roast mushroom?' asked Sarah of her mother and sister.

'I don't feel like that. I'm sorry. I just don't want a "roast mushroom with pickled red cabbage and potatoes" for lunch,' replied Polly.

'They don't even have any chicken,' said his mother.

'Let's leave now. We don't have to stay. If you're not going to eat, we can just go,' said Sarah.

'Don't get upset. I don't mind sitting here. It's perfectly pleasant to be here with the children. They're enjoying themselves. I'll eat later,' said his mother.

'What a happy and easy-going family we are,' said Water. 'Why don't you just order something? I'll eat it if you can't.'

Eventually his mother and sister both agreed to have roast mushrooms. And another waiter said the kitchen could find some sausages and penne with tomato sauce for the children.

What arrived was a wedge of green-tinged chicken liver pâté, which Water had insisted on having as a starter, followed by some sourly rancid lamb, sausages which contained a little rotten pork, and mushrooms originally cooked the day before swilling in gravy and with cauliflower cheese as an accompaniment.

Ugly food.

Water's family left most of the food on their plates. Even Sarah's boyfriend, when questioned, admitted that his rare-breed roast pork was 'a bit tough'.

'You shouldn't pay for this,' said his mother to Frances, whose treat it was.

'I don't want to make a scene. I might want to come here for a drink one day; it's in my neighbourhood,' replied Frances. Water thought it an unassertive response from a barrister.

'Don't pay for a side salad for me. They never brought it,' said Water.

'I won't,' answered Frances.

'How much did this "food" cost?' asked Polly.

'Forget about it. Let's just go,' said Frances.

They left to have the birthday cake at Frances's. There, in the garden, they sat together, his sisters and mother joking and talking, Water reading the paper, contributing the occasional remark, the children playing, and the dog eating leftover cake from a paper plate. When he got home he wrote an email to Eliane asking whether she had fallen in love with him yet. He wrote that he would be devastated if there was to be no romance between them. He told her that it was better to be his mistress than his friend, because all his women friends fell in love with him eventually, which was tragic as he believed in the sanctity of friendship. And he said that it was natural to take a lover when you were married: in Italy you didn't even wait till after the ceremony. Water couldn't even picture this blonde Belgian girl (woman, he corrected himself, she was nearly twenty-four). He felt no physical desire for his memory of her, although perhaps she had had pretty eyes. So he wrote to her because he was bored and the inexorable logic of his personality commanded him to do so. She wrote back the next day that she didn't think she wanted to be his mistress, or anyone else's for that matter.

48

Thinking.

When Water was eight he fell in love with a blonde girl in his class at school. She was tall and American. And perhaps Water had liked her because she reminded him of the place he had been born and left only a few years before. He dreamt of her then. He was too scared to talk to her, and it would be years before he worked out what to say. Often when he met women he would be reminded of that first recognition of love. Her name was Olivia. He wished they could have kissed. It would have better than all the kisses he had had afterwards, most of which he had forgotten. He could not remember much of what he had done. There had been days in his entire history – days which defined periods in his memory – where he had felt an overwhelming sexual attraction, but they were rare. And often, if he remembered carefully, that passion had followed a lengthy period of abstinence which had caused a buildup of desire. Water had slept with more than half of all the women he had kissed. He thought this showed him to be persistent. He regretted the time he had wasted when he was younger, when he was self-conscious rather than self-aware. His friends did not believe that he had ever been less than prodigiously confident. Certainly his success had developed so quickly as to obliterate what had preceded it. But there were a few years when he had not been able to do and know exactly what he had wanted. Now he faced a world where he was the leader; what he thought, happened. Sex and love could only be repeated. Water thought that the person who said 'repetition was happiness' was wrong. There would not be a woman he met, fell in love with and spent the rest of his life with. The prospect of such a woman had in itself become awful. He imagined he and this woman sitting around talking, laughing, eating dinner together, having sex, waking up, eating breakfast, going to work, coming back. Then he wished she would go home. Even as a fantasy he was exhausted by the strain of such happiness. He thought: Harriet was such a woman and I grew to hate her, leaving her just when it was all perfect (he edited out her loss of the baby, for some reason). The woman I've now married, Jelena, I hate, and that allows me to continue with her. She thinks she loves me, but she doesn't because otherwise I would really hate her. Jelena wants me to love her. She doesn't love me. That is why she is so terrible. That is why I can stand her. That's why I couldn't stand Harriet or any other woman.

Water thought: my intention, when I was younger, was to be successful. Being successful involved having good (that is beautiful, strong, intelligent) girlfriends. I presumed I would also have a wife and children at some point. I knew that family was important even when I was young, that if you lost them or tried to go it alone, you became sad and weak. Now I have been married twice. I will not leave Jelena. Once is enough. Yet I have no faith in my marriage to her. In all this I feel no sense of failure and very little guilt. I would not have done very much differently, to change one part of it would degrade my ecstatic love of every aspect of my existence. Those who could be said to have been damaged by my actions made their own choices for their own reasons. And I don't believe they wish they had never met me. Water wondered whether this was how evildoers had always justified their actions, but he could not shake off the feeling that he had done nothing wrong.

With each show he did, Water realized that he was further away from being certain that his paintings were important. Yet the heroes in the books he read were always aware of their fallibility and absurdity, and still chose to prevail. The artists who had killed themselves, the revolutionaries who had grown paranoid, the people who kept grudges too long, the men and women who hated themselves, had made a mistake in forgetting that this life was all they had. He thought.

49

Friends' birthdays. The hell of fun.

Suddenly all his friends turned thirty. Their parties came when he was already old with a house, ex-wife, wife, and baby on the way. He was not yet thirty. Mary's party was in the country, in one of those dead counties that surround London. Mary's parents owned a big weekend house with a tennis court, swimming pool and croquet lawn. He remembered going there when he was twenty, at the time he had still been interested in knowing more about his friends so it had been a thrill to spend a weekend with them. This time was different: all the same people, just a little uglier, with less to say, every one he knew enough to know he would know no more of, nor wanted to. He had thought it would be dull, and when he arrived late, with two friends he had brought as insurance, they were all there chatting in one of the converted barns. His fears were confirmed.

The plan had been to arrive early so that Water could play tennis all afternoon, making himself energized enough to bear the evening. But Michael (the same Michael he had once tried to get rid of at openings) had been late picking him up, claiming that he had lost his keys, though Water suspected he had been watching cricket on the TV.

It had been a terrible drive, with Michael overtaking every car he could and raging at any delays they encountered. It made Water wish he could drive. He still owned a car that he couldn't drive because he never had enough time to complete his lessons.

'Hello, Mrs Paul,' said Water to Mary's mother.

'Hello Water! I'm so happy you could come. Where is Jelena? Is she in Slo ... Slovenia?'

'Yes. She's back in Slovenia. She has to stay in bed until the baby is born. I brought my two friends, David and Dan, instead.'

Slovenia. The mail often goes there by mistake.

Mrs P began asking Michael and Dan about themselves, and Water went off to find Mary.

'Hello Mary, happy birthday,' he said, shaking hands with her. Water's greetings were particular to each person. He usually didn't kiss hello women with whom he had had possibilities of romance, though he made an exception for Italians, and he also kissed ex-girlfriends.

'Hi, Water. Lovely to see you.'

'Lovely,' echoed Water.

'How's Jelena?'

'She's OK. The baby's still inside her, so I can go to a few more parties before I have to start changing nappies.'

'I hope she's all right.'

'I brought you a painting as a present, but if you're not going to appreciate it, I'm not going to give it to you.'

'You don't want me to have it?'

'Only if you're going to like it.'

'I'm sure I will,' she said, and apologized for having to go off, and went.

Water hated giving people paintings as gifts; they never appreciated how valuable they were, but he was most often too lazy to buy them something.

He looked around at his thirty-year-old friends chatting over canapés (smoked salmon, sushi, mini-quiches and cherry tomatoes and tiny mozzarellas on sticks). He thought of Larkin saying (so he had been quoted on a TV documentary) that between twenty and forty was the fillet steak of life, the rest was the scrag ends. It looked like the game was up for his friends: they were already offal. He wished that the pretty converted barn would burn down, and that these apparitions of dull middle age might become real and run shrieking into the night, leaving their dire boring fates behind. What questions could he care to ask these people. How's your job? Where are you living? Have you got a partner? What are you doing this summer? They would congratulate him on his wedding and baby, ask where his wife was, ignore his achievements in painting and move on to talk with someone they felt more comfortable with. It was only 6.30pm, and as it was a sleepover party there was not even the prospect of it ending soon.

'Hello, Water.' It was James, another old friend of Water's from college. James could be very funny, but Water knew that it would be draining to keep up the witty banter with him. Those who had studied at Oxford or Cambridge never relaxed in their efforts to be clever, or at least prove they were more ironic than anyone else.

'Hello, Jim,' replied Water, even though no one called him Jim.

'How's married life?'

'Not much different from single life, except people keep asking me that.'

'Where's your beautiful wife?'

'She's back in Slovenia.'

'I thought she was Serbian.' James turned to his girlfriend, whose name Water had forgotten again.

'Water told me he was going out with the most beautiful woman in the world. And that she was a supermodel.'

'I never said she was a supermodel. I said she looked like a supermodel. Anyway, you saw her; she does.'

'Whatever,' answered James in an American accent.

James's girlfriend spoke up. 'She is beautiful. Don't be horrible, James.'

'Don't worry about it. James is always rude about my girlfriends, then he tries to sleep with them.'

'There's no need to be so aggressive,' James said, looking embarrassed.

Water left them to get a drink, but instead exited the barn and went for a walk in the garden. It was still light outside. In the gravel driveway were a selection of small cars, alongside Mary's parents' Jaguar and Mercedes. The house, he thought, might be pretty, with its clematis and ivy and its surrounding lawns and hedges, and little river and thatched barns. But somehow it was just a big pile of ugly bricks. The party went on, Water constantly looking at his mobile phone to check what time it was, hoping it might be late enough for him to go to bed. The guests drank champagne, wine, beer, vodka, gin, tonic; they snorted cocaine, swam, danced to disco music, and it all just made them paler and more tired-looking. Water went into the pool, and someone playfully threw a football at him, which smacked him on his neck. The water's reflections made the trees dance in the black of the country night. When more people arrived and made to take their clothes off for a midnight skinny-dip, Water hurried off inside, claiming he was too cold to stay in any longer. He remembered his excitement years before at being in the water with the girls from college, naked! Now he couldn't face seeing his friends' and acquaintances' bodies in the flesh; the images would stick in his head.

After changing into warm clothes, he went to sit out the rest of the party in the kitchen of the main house. People came and went, looking for food, or partners, or prospective partners. Some lingered to talk to him, some he insulted in passing. All seemed to be looking for what they couldn't find. They were missing happiness, Water thought, sitting in his armchair next to the drinks cabinet. Finally at 3.30am, he mustered the strength to find a duvet and fall asleep on the sofa in the less fancy sitting room. The party had been winding down almost since it began, but the occasional noisy conversation still broke his sleep. After a long dreaming night he could sleep no longer, and emerged to find out it was 11.30am and a new day was upon him.

'Hello, good morning,' he said to Mary's mother, who had spent the night at a cousin's house nearby.

'Did you have a nice night?'

'It was OK. I wish you'd stayed. We needed some more interesting women.'

'I'm sure there were plenty of lovely people about.'

'They're all too young for me to talk too. I'm a married man.' Water was enjoying talking nonsense. 'What's for breakfast?' he continued. The large kitchen was full of people he hadn't had anything to say to the previous night.

'Help yourself. There's plenty of bread and cheese from last night,' Mary's mother said, which Water thought was a poor effort; they could have at least supplied a proper breakfast. He took a Coke out of the fridge and announced he was going to play tennis until he was really hungry. No one paid him much heed. Even Mary's mother had lost her old interest in feeding him. Perhaps he was losing his ability to charm his friends' mothers.

The sun was shining hot for once, and he could feel it burning his bare back. Water was not good at tennis, not county standard, hadn't played for his school (no one had, as they didn't compete against other schools at any sports), hadn't had any lessons, wasn't a member of a club and didn't play in a league. But he was better than other players who weren't good.

'I haven't lost for ten years,' he shouted at the blue sky, and smacked the ground with his racquet repeatedly. It wasn't true; a few years before he had lost 6–1, 6–0 to a guy who knew what he was doing. He had decided then never to play anyone good again.

'You're fucking Spanish pussies,' he told his friends, the pleasant Spanish couple he was playing against.

He made himself be over-competitive. It made the game more fun. He forced people to care whether they won. And he was good at winning because he was relentless. If he lost one set, he would say best of three. If an opponent had a bad backhand, he hit every shot there.

'I'm not going to lose a match today. I'm going to beat every single fucking pussy here,' said Water, in a voice he thought sounded a bit like Al Pacino.

After two hours of doubles, where each time he chose the

worst partner to underline his singular superiority, he was still unbeaten, and elated from the sunshine and exercise. He went for a swim, and thought that in a few years he should retire to a house with a pool and tennis courts, and that he was happy and would be happy with that.

'Is there any French bread? I can't eat this brown stuff,' said Water to the people eating bread and cheese.

He was an obnoxious child, facetious as his father would say, but it didn't seem to matter. Those who were sensitive he had offended years ago.

'You're so revolting, Water.'

He cut a Port Salut in two and placed the larger of the pieces on a piece of bread.

'I suppose this will have to do,' he said. 'Who wants to play football with me?' he asked.

No one answered.

'No one. You're all fucking lazy.'

'You seem to be full of energy,' someone noted.

'I'm an athlete, my body is a machine. I need to exercise it. I can't just sit around reading the Sunday newspapers and eating cheese and fucking brown bread all day. You people have something wrong with you.'

The target of his assault smiled at his ranting, and turned back to the paper.

'God, you're all dead. Who wants to play tennis? Come on, James. I'll beat you.'

'No. I'm not playing. We're leaving soon. I want to go to the garden centre on the way back.'

'The garden centre? How middle-aged are you?'

'You can't get such good plants in London,' replied James.

'Unbelievable,' said Water, and walked off in mock anger, back to the tennis court.

Following more tennis and swimming, Water was satisfied. He had managed to destroy his graphite tennis racquet somehow.

'Goodbye.'

'Bye-bye.'

'See you soon.'

'Safe journey.'

'I'll be expecting you to send me a replacement tennis racquet. Thanks for the party,' shouted Water. And they drove away, their tires crunching on the gravel driveway.

'Are we going to stop for a hamburger on the way back?' asked Water. He was sitting in front with Michael. Dan was quiet in the back. The music, early Beatles, was on loud. They had finished the m&ms.

'You mean McDonalds? It's disgusting. I won't eat there,' replied Michael.

'I love it. So does Bill Clinton. You can't beat a cheeseburger. Or a Big Mac for that matter. A good McDonalds is as good as anything,' said Water.

'If you like eating complete shit.'

'It's not shit. You're fucking shit. It's the most advanced food there is. Try and make a cheeseburger, like a McDonalds one, at home.'

'I wouldn't want to. Anyway, you know what they do with their factories, and their meat, and their workers. It's the most evil company in the world. You only like it to be annoying and ironic.'

'I never realized you were a hippy.'

They fell silent. Water was uncomfortable because Michael liked to drive with the windows shut. And the car was stuffy with the three of them in it, and his back was sweaty against the seat, and he felt like a hamburger, and not having Michael moaning about him eating it.

They approached a service station with a Burger King and Water thought to mention it to Michael. They were quickly past

it, and the red car in front of them seemed not to be moving. Water considered telling Michael that they were going to hit the red car if their car carried on in a straight line. Then they were about to drive into the back of the red car. Then they hit it and there was not a huge smash. Just a very hard strike of car against car. Water was thrown forward. His seatbelt restrained him. The red car was shot forward by the impact. Their car stopped. Along the road were bits of broken plastic. The only damage to the red car seemed to be a broken rear light. Their car's front was caved in.

'What happened?'

'Is everyone OK?'

'That other car wasn't moving.'

'Maybe we should get out?'

Dan, Michael and Water exited their car, and from the other car a fat man in towelling shorts approached them.

'What happened?' he asked.

'Are you all right?' David asked.

'My wife's a bit shaken up.' She remained in the car, invisible.

'Perhaps you should get the car off the road, Michael,' said Water.

Michael drove the car onto the motorway verge. He and the other man then exchanged details, not realizing there was more to having a crash than that. Water felt a small wrench in his shoulder and neck. When he rolled up his trouser leg there was a small cut on his knee with a delicate trickle of blood coming from it. It must have jammed against the jagged plastic on the glove compartment. The blood had stained his white trousers.

A policeman arrived and a long drawn-out process began of breath tests, skid measuring and forms to be filled in. Then the AA and the tow trucks had to be waited for. Water asked the policeman how they were meant to get home. He replied it was not his business. Water went off to eat a hamburger at Burger King, and by the time he had returned, James had stopped with his car full of plants.

'Lucky you stopped. Can you take us back to London?' said Water.

'It's too full. I don't think I can take three people in the car. I might be able to take one person,' he said.

'Michael will go with the tow truck, so it's only two.'

'I'm not sure. I haven't driven much lately.'

'So what are we meant to do? Can't you put the plants in the boot?' said Water.

James's girlfriend looked embarrassed but stayed silent.

'I'll try, but isn't there anyone else who could take you?' said James.

'No.'

Back in London, James dropped the accident victims at a tube stop an hour from Water's house.

In bed that night Water wondered whether he would have nightmares.

50

With a woman I don't remember.

Eliane, O Eliane, when will you fall in love with me? Water texted to Eliane. She replied that he was married and that she couldn't fall in love with a married man. Why not? Because it was too complicated. She wanted one hundred per cent love. 'But you have fallen a little in love with me?' he emailed her.

'No. I am just intrigued by you.'

'What's there to be intrigued by?' he replied, interested in what she might admire about him.

'You are funny, and your situation is funny. You behave like a little kid when you don't get what you want.'

'I want you.' He thought that might be overstating matters, but it was the best reply. She answered,

'You're married and you've got a kid on the way and you're just not ready to settle down yet, and you're fighting it by pursuing me.' He loved the way she could be so prosaic.

'Eliane, I was thinking of you this morning.'

'What were you thinking, Water?'

'You sure you want to know?' he asked, with the coyness that was a standard feature of flirtation, but made him feel a little sleazy. 'I was hoping you had big breasts.'

'I have little titties.'

'I like those too (two).'

'Fuck off,' she replied.

'Why?'

'You just burst the bubble.'

'Why?'

'I am not in the mood.'

'Why?'

'Sexist.'

'I was just showing my real self,' he replied.

'Goodbye.'

'I apologize for offending you.'

'You ruined it. Bye.'

'OK I'm sorry.'

'Don't apologize. Bye.'

'Ciao.' 'Can I make up for it?'

'No.'

'I'll send you some flowers.'

'No. Bye.'

'OK Goodbye.'

So he communicated with a woman in Belgium via emails and texts. They told each other how many people they had slept with, what they liked to eat, when they had lost their virginity, what pets they had had as children, and many other details. Their exchange was more about information than romance. She looked him up on a search engine and found his paintings, which she liked. She sent him some photos by email of her at a party dressed as a flapper, on holiday in Los Angeles, and drunk in a bar in Brussels with a guy who had been her boyfriend. In some of the pictures she looked pretty, a bit like Lauren Bacall when she was young, and in some she looked bug-eyed and not that great. He emailed her a photo of him in his studio that he thought showed him looking quite cool.

She forgave him for desiring, in his imagination, that her breasts were large. Water had forgotten at some point that women never took kindly to comments about how their bodies could be improved. A girlfriend had once asked him how he'd like it if she told him his penis was too small. But it wasn't quite the same; it was more like women saying they liked tall men. Very annoying if you were a short man, but he didn't like short men either, they always seemed to have something to prove. Also you couldn't say it was definitely negative to be short or have small breasts, surely it was a matter of taste. Water thought, the problem with me is that, like my father, I can never admit that I'm wrong, and that is a very bad thing in the long run. I call myself a feminist, and I am, as my sisters have often said, the biggest sexist around.

Eliane was not sure why she cared what Water thought of her. He had only met her twice in his life, and she didn't even think he was her type. He was probably not quite tall enough for her, and she remembered him with quite a fat face. Though, as she was not in love with anyone else and needed distraction, he was interesting. She had also just split up with a man who she had thought was going to be perfect. He had been English as well, a musician, but it had ended when she went to visit him in Paris where he lived. He had told her he felt claustrophobic and had been very cold from the moment she arrived. They had met at a club in Brussels where his band was playing. She saw his face on a video screen, and thought, 'Wow, who is this guy?' Then later she had been dancing, and he looked at her, and she must have looked back at him in the same way, and he walked over and kissed her. The next morning she had to get up early, and he had to go back to Paris. But they sent each other very passionate emails, and he visited a couple of times, and she saw him when his band was playing nearby. He said she should come to Paris, so one day, with her laptop and not much stuff, she did. It didn't work but at least she had tried. Eliane wanted to be totally in love. She thought it was the best feeling in the world, though maybe she should avoid English men in future; they seemed quite fucked up.

As Water sat at his computer, hoping Eliane would be online soon, he thought, I am a ridiculous man who cannot take no for an answer. For me, no is the beginning of all desire. It was my first word when I was a baby. Though if you asked my mother she would probably say it was something else. The whole of our lives are based on contradiction. My second wife is about to give birth, and she is far away, and my paintings are hanging in the Tate, yet my main preoccupation is whether this stupid Belgian girl will fall in love with me. If she did, what would I do? Take the Eurostar to Brussels and take her to a movie then fuck her? Then what? She would want me like she wanted her previous English boyfriend, and I would run a mile or a thousand miles. I suppose my hope is to keep it all in a state of flux, so I can imagine the delicious possibilities of romance and deception without really doing much. Yet I am not any more a faithful person, except to myself, so I should stop caring and just enjoy what happens. That's what Water thought.

Eliane was making carrot and coriander soup. It was a boring afternoon, too hot for her to concentrate on the article she was meant to be writing. And she didn't feel like the soup she was making; it was just something to do. She thought about Chris, the English musician in Paris, and wanted to send him a text message to see how he was, but thought that would be pointless. Instead she connected to the internet to find out what Water was doing.

When Water saw the message from Eliane pop up on his computer screen, he was pleased. So she's still interested, he thought. Hello W, it said. He didn't reply. He was tired of this Belgian woman before he had even begun an affair with her. He didn't need another woman to tell him that what he said was nasty. Although he wasn't yet thirty he knew that he would not stop being a rude and aggressive person, and that the more it was pointed out to him that he should be nicer the worse he got. He hated being told what to do, and what not to say. He would say anything he fucking felt like.

Eliane, he was sure, was a victim of many traumatic experiences and the usual self-loathing about her figure. Water, in the end, and with due acknowledgement of his shallowness, liked medium to large breasts more than he liked small ones. Although breast size was, of course, never (he was not a Neanderthal, after all) the ultimate determining factor in his attraction towards a woman. He also didn't like people who got upset easily; he preferred an argument to sad disappointment from the offended party. Another message from Eliane appeared. 'Radio Silence?' it asked. He thought, no not silence; just another example of something boring concluded. And he shut down his computer with satisfaction.

51

It ends whimpering. It's amazing how you can ignore all the big good things, while parties, openings, boring girls keep you busy.

His friend Adam approached. Water pretended he was engrossed in conversation with the friends he was standing with. People were on the street because the gallery was small. The crowd outside made the opening seem quite a success. The gallery was just an old shop with letters on the windows spelling out the exhibiting artists' names. Water felt obliged to go see the show because it included an old friend from Rome. He could not remember a time when he had ever seen a good piece of art in any low-budget exhibition. Never in all the shows he had been to. He hadn't seen anything good in so long, he had ceased to even consider it a possibility that he might. All these galleries were tragic. They made no money and exhibited nothing but emptiness, and they contained the dreams and work of so many artists. Like artists, a few of the little ones became big, real dealers with proper galleries where art was sold, but it was too small a percentage to be significant.

'Hello Water,' said Adam to Water, who managed to avoid eye contact with him until the last possible moment.

'Hello, you bastard,' replied Water, in a tone of affectionate good humour.

As Adam didn't speak, Water continued. 'So you didn't make my wedding party. Didn't phone, didn't send a card. Nothing. And no present either.'

'We've been really busy. I'm sorry. We had to get the preliminary drawings in. We've been working every weekend, and haven't had any time. I'm really sorry.'

'What are you working on?' asked Water.

'The school. Still on the commission to redesign the school.'

'It's not good enough. It's over, buddy. It was my fucking wedding. Sometimes friendships come to an end. You have to make an effort. I have given you lots of chances. I thought we were friends. You could have bloody called. Anyway it's enough,' said Water, whose mood had quickly turned dark.

'I understand.' It was hard to tell whether Adam was upset or just embarrassed. Water had often said things, especially in front of Adam's wife, that had made him look uncomfortable. But Water had genuinely been surprised by Adam's lack of loyalty.

'So I hope it all goes well for you. Maybe in a few years we can be friends again. *Arrivederci.*'

'Yeah. Maybe. Goodbye,' said Adam, and walked into the gallery to find his wife.

Water turned back to his friends, the anger gone from his face and his cheery countenance restored for their benefit.

Later, after he had drunk more, someone asked whether he was upset.

'You look really sad,' she said.

'I'm fine. I hate it when I'm told I look depressed; it makes me wonder whether I am.'

'I was just worried about you.'

'That's nice of you. I was thinking about what I said to Adam earlier. He didn't show up for my wedding party. He didn't send a present. And he didn't even bother to call to apologize. Nothing. It was fucking rude. When I can't go to a wedding I at least send a card or something. It's not about a present. I don't care about presents. What do I want? But I need my friends to show me love. So I told him that it was over, to forget that I was his friend. I think he was a bit surprised. But I don't care. He didn't show me any love,' said Water.

'You need love,' she said.

'We all do. I like that expression, show me the love. I want my friends to show me love. It's true. I don't care whether they are complete fucking losers, or crazy, or never pay for a drink. But I need some loyalty. Like those who came to Venice to see my show, they showed me their love.'

'You sound like that guy from *Jerry Maguire* who says "show me the money, show me the money",' she said.

Water laughed. He shouted 'Show me the love, show me the fucking love.' Maybe that was from the film, too. He didn't care. It was a summer evening, the kind that always filled him with exuberance, and he had released some of his rage in his conversation with Adam. He had been right to do that, Water thought.

'Are you also nervous about your new responsibilities?' she asked.

'What responsibilities? You mean being a father?'

'Yes. It's a very big change.'

'I'm looking forward to it. It's not difficult being a father. I sent Jelena a platinum MasterCard, so she's happy. Now I don't need to worry until the kid goes to school.'

'You're awful.'

'People keep going on at me about responsibility. It's great to have a baby. It's not about responsibility, like getting a mortgage or a pension. It's a happy event, not some boring responsibility. I hate these fucking people who are already planning which organic school to send their kids to before they're even born. I like children.'

'You sound positive about it.'

'It's just sinking in. Last night I had a dream about my daughter. It was the first time the idea has come up in my subconscious or dream conscious, or whatever. When I dream about something, it's like a rehearsal. It means I really have taken it in.'

'A month before the birth!'

'I don't like to worry too much in advance. I take one day at a time.'

'Did I tell you that dream I had about you?' she asked.

'I haven't finished telling you about mine. Anyway, there's nothing worse than hearing about other people's dreams. My mother always says, write it down in your diary. So I'll make it short. She, my daughter in the dream, was really beautiful. And she was eating with a fork, and I couldn't believe it because she was so young. I was thinking my daughter was a genius, really intelligent, and I was really happy in the dream.'

'I once dreamt I was giving birth, and I think I was in the sea. There was a storm and boats all around,' she replied.

Water had stopped listening.

When he got home he called Jelena.

'Hi. How are you?' Water asked.

'Fine.'

'And how's the baby?'

'OK.'

'So you're in a good mood.'

'I can't sleep.'

'That's good, you can read a lot.'

'It gives me a headache to read too much.'

'So what are you doing?'

'Nothing. Lying here. What have you been doing?'

'Nothing. Painting. I went to an opening this evening. It was boring. Then I had a drink with some friends and came home.'

'Which friends?'

'Just some boring people. Adam was there.'

'Adam?'

'You met him in Rome.'

'Why do you spend all your time with those losers?' Jelena asked.

'Which losers?'

'Your friends. Who you buy drinks for and listen to their stupid problems.'

'Always so charming.'

'You help all those idiots, while I am here alone with your child.'

'What are you talking about? You're with your parents.'

'When I go to the hospital they say where is your husband. Everyone asks where you are. I am alone, and when you call me you make me feel more alone and miserable. Stop calling me.'

'OK. Well, I hope you are OK.'

'Goodbye. Don't call me.'

'Bye,' he said, and hung up.

Water was disappointed that he had not been able to tell Jelena his dream.

52

The career triumphs. The baby is born. The novel ends.

The reviews said that his show was a disappointment. It's not that they said that, just that they didn't say it was brilliant. A few spoke of hubris and bubbles bursting. Water didn't care that much. His name was outside the Serpentine and each letter of 'Nathaniel Water' was at least two feet wide or high. It would have been a bonus if it had been loved. Perhaps he had gone too far by filling one room with copies, made by him, of paintings he had done when he was at school. He had wanted to see if there was a real difference between his juvenile efforts and his so-called mature work. He liked the risk of showing paintings that people might reject because an adult had not done them. Stupid people sometimes said his work was childlike, now they could see for themselves whether it was or it wasn't, or anyway he was blurring some boundary by merging the two. After all that had happened in art, Water was amazed that childlike was still even used as a criticism.

Another old-fashioned idea was that a painting needed a certain amount of work in it to make it worthwhile. Even curators, gallerists and collectors still found it hard to accept art, especially paintings, which looked careless or unfinished. Water thought the history of painting progressed always to paintings that looked more and more unfinished, from Constable to Manet to the Impressionists to Pollock, each generation had been accused of making a mess and insulting the public with their lack of effort. Water thought the big crime in art was that of labour, that look of hours spent in the studio by an artist with no ideas churning out a nicely finished product – the same one over and over again, in neatly applied colours, which had been carefully mixed and applied with the correct brush, while the brainless artist listened to the radio and used the same concepts they had originally been fed at art school many years before.

So in the final gallery he had shown new paintings which had taken him about fifteen minutes each to paint. How long did they take you? A typical dumb question. He would answer, 'About fifteen minutes.' Fifteen minutes of painting was not necessarily worse than fifteen hours or fifteen days. How could it be? Water liked that there was a small possibility that viewers might spend longer looking at his painting than he had spent painting them.

His show at The Serpentine was titled 'To the Happy Few'. Water had been allowed near-total control over the project, from the catalogue to how the pictures were hung. He had decided to do exactly what he wanted without any compromises. Water sensed that his power might have peaked for the time being, and he was determined to make the most of it. He thought his retrospective (they called it a survey and were right because the gallery wasn't big enough for a proper retrospective) was brilliant. He had found the opening tiring and not that glamorous. Jelena had been unable to come, of course, and he was sure she would have ruined it in some way if she had been there, but without her it was missing part of the triumph. Many women there showed signs of attraction towards him. He found them ugly and English. He hoped perhaps to meet a new beautiful charming woman, but none came.

His giant family turned up and stood together, to be admired and only approached by the brave or curious. He was rich and famous. His mother seemed proud. His father was in America. Afterwards there was a party in a private club.

In Slovakia, or Slovenia, Jelena was in hospital. Water arrived on the day the papers in England printed photos of the minor celebrities at his opening. He read Dickens in the empty waiting room outside the labour ward because Jelena didn't want him to see her give birth, or because she told him that the doctors would only let you if you had special hygienic shoes and had done a training course. He read three hundred pages of *David Copperfield*, and hated it. The hospital was not so bad, green and grey, no worse than England. The cafeteria, which was closed now, served quite nice food. He hated Jelena, but he knew that was just because he felt left out. Her mother was with her (she had the right shoes) and every so often she would push out of the heavy swing doors and say, 'OK?' She knew he was not. He tried to remember his show, his success and his life. He felt guilty for not being more excited, or more concerned for Jelena. After six hours, he was allowed in. There was blood, and metal bowls. Her mother smiled nervously. Jelena was pale, lying on a vinyl bed. She said they had had to cut her. A nurse was weighing the baby. When she was done, his daughter was offered to him.

I divorce Jelena.